This book is dedicated to the wonderful ladies on our ARC and Promo team–you are amazing!

·

Special thanks to Ginny at AZ Editing.

·

Thanks also goes to Leni Kauffman who continues to capture Jane perfectly.

·

Much love to Naomi Lane for, well, EVERYTHING

CHAPTER ONE

"Never say you'll cross *any* line to win. Not out loud."
Jane Ladling, Cemetery Girl

Jane Ladling lived by three rules. Well, two rules and a strong suggestion. Or semi-strong, bordering on incredibly soft. 1. Never fall in love. 2. Always be good to pets, family, and friends. And 3. Absolutely, under no circumstances, break rule number one.

Currently, she stood on a makeshift stage, shoulder to shoulder with her best friend and confidant, Fiona Lawrence, smiling and waving at party guests. Jane kept those rules front and center as her gaze continued to stray to a certain Georgia Bureau of Homicide Special Agent. No more than twenty feet away, he engaged in deep conversation with a rapt circle of townspeople eager to learn more about a recent case. The Woeful Widow and Mr. Art Amour. Solved by Jane herself, thank you very much.

The romantic setting didn't help her endeavor. Soft music played in the background of a large, transparent tent with plastic walls. A structure that dominated the entrance to her landlocked cemetery, Garden of Memories. Moonlight and stars glowed overhead while a hint of magnolia and jasmine scented the air, soon to fade until the return of spring. Along the outside perimeter, trees swayed with a gentle fall breeze. Within, lanterns flickered with hazy light, illuminating gold and black balloon arches and twirling streamers. White pumpkins and glittery pinecones added a taste of autumn.

The roaring twenties themed soiree was in full swing.

"Mmm mmm mmm." Fiona gave Jane a gentle nudge. "I see you're as riveted to that boy's hot buttered buns as I am."

"Oh my gosh." Caught staring! "We shouldn't discuss his, um, derriere." Jane's cheeks flushed as she slid her gaze over Conrad Ryan for the thousandth time that evening. He wore a white button-down with dark slacks and a matching jacket, perfectly fitted to his lean, muscular frame. "But you aren't wrong. Those buns are *sizzling*, aren't they?"

Fiona fanned her cheeks. "I can feel the burn from here."

Once, the sixty-two-year-old had been like a sister to Jane's Grandma Lily. When the darling woman passed, Fiona became Jane's rock. Despite their thirty-six-year age difference, they were like sisters, too.

"He should wear a sign," Jane said. "Handle with care."

As if he sensed the scrutiny, Conrad cast a glance over one broad shoulder. Thank goodness she looked up in time to catch his eye. He winked before refacing his audience.

But that was all it took. Jane's breath caught and her heart thudded. Dang, he was beautiful. Tall and strong, with thick black hair, and whiskey-colored irises. A straight nose and firm jaw added to his incomparable appeal. The Rolex on his wrist hid the tattoos that peaked from the sleeves of his jacket.

The day they'd met, the Atlanta native had come to her hometown, and all but accused her of murdering a doctor. Since then, he'd wreaked complete havoc on Aurelian Hills—

and her life! Perhaps not as much havoc as she'd wreaked upon his, but that was neither here nor there. Now they were kinda, sorta, well, dating. If you could date someone without going on actual dates with them. Which sounded weird. But hey, welcome to Jane's world.

When you owned and operated an ancestral cemetery, weird became the norm. Besides, she and Conrad had enjoyed something a million times better than romantic dinners or trips to the theater. They solved murders together! Two so far.

Although, granted, Jane had done the bulk of the solving. Not that she was bragging or anything. Truth was truth. Conrad's problem? He relied on clues and logic. Meanwhile, Jane utilized a far superior method. Conjecture. Everybody kept secrets. Suspect the worst from the beginning and work from there. Sure, she had no friends outside her inner circle, but who needed more of those when you had such an amazing assortment of confidants?

She ignored the sudden spike of longing that constricted her chest.

Anyway. Despite the special agent's lack of imagination, he'd somehow wormed his way into her heart. Just the outer layer, though! Not the gooey center, where love bubbled and brewed. She would never, never, *ever* let herself love him. Or anyone! Break rule number one? No!

Her personal code had developed from a family curse. Like, a legit curse. But it only affected the women. Fall in love, lose the guy. An outcome as certain as death. Her mom had lost her dad. Grandma Lily had lost Pops. Her great grandmother Opal lost a husband twice! And on and on and on.

Not happening to me. Nope. Jane had lost too much already.

"How do I look?" Fiona asked, adjusting her costume. "To die for?"

Jane gave the gorgeous "Nana" a once-over. With Fiona's salt-and-pepper hair pinned back, she put her dark, unlined skin on display. A drop-waisted gown highlighted a buxom figure. The cloche hat and long string of pearls completed the outfit.

"You steal my breath," Jane said with a smile. "See what I did there?"

They shared a snicker.

To pad Jane's meager family trust—among other reasons —she'd teamed up with the town's premiere party planners, Charlotte and Audrey Berdize, to kick off Aurelian Hill's first murder mystery party. The Case of the Hotsy-Totsy Bandit. Beyond this point, inside the cemetery itself, local businesses had set up booths to advertise, display and sell their goods and services while handing out clues. Including the Berdize sisters.

"Honestly, Fee, you look like you stepped from a picture of the 1920s," Jane added. "Classic. Timeless. Lovely."

Her friend preened. "I gotta say, you took the words right out of my mouth about you, hon. You are classic, timeless, and lovely as well."

"I am, aren't I?" Jane responded with a teasing smile, fluffing her coiffed hair. After days of deliberation, she'd chosen a gold flapper dress, with dotted tulle and feathers. On her head perched a glorious fascinator hat. Both the fascinator and the cloche belonged to her extensive—and impressive—collection.

A buzz sounded from her phone, letting her know she'd gotten a new text. She sighed. No need to read the screen. She knew the message came from a Berdize sister. The pair had been reaching out every two minutes or so.

Jane checked–yep. Sure enough.

A-Berdize: *Why haven't you released the hounds into the wild already????*

The guests were the hounds, she assumed. Her gaze strayed to the clock in the upper left hand of the screen. 8:16 p.m. She heaved another sigh. It wasn't her fault the MC was late, preventing the players from receiving their first clue.

Rather than explain, she replied with a shrug emoji. Invited fewer questions.

As she returned the device to her pocket, a man in the corner snagged her attention. Anthony Miller, draining the contents of a flask, glaring at someone in the crowd. Jane stiffened. Had her former lawyer come to demand more money she didn't owe him?

Fiona patted her hand. "Don't you worry, dear. Sheriff Moore will be here in a hop, skip and a jump. Why, I bet he went to check on his deputies. They're patrolling the city without him tonight and I think we can both agree he's the brains in that operation. Once he starts emcee-ing, everyone will forget the wait. They'll be too enraptured by his delicious voice to remember."

Sheriff Moore. A gruff protector had stolen Fiona's affections. Obviously.

Though Jane considered the man's voice, well, normal, she said, "I hope you're right, Fee." Conrad's voice on the other hand…

"Besides," Fiona continued, unfazed. "No one seems to mind the wait. Everyone is having a wonderful time."

Excitement *did* crackle all around. At small, round tables, children painted mini-treasure boxes. Costumed adults gobbled up hors d'oeuvres, drank champagne, and snapped photos in front of a giant Wanted poster featuring Beau Harden, another childhood friend of Jane's. More than half the town had shown up, paying fifty bucks a pop to try to solve the elaborate murder she'd crafted herself. And, okay, yes, everyone also hoped to win a weekend stay at the newly opened Aurelian Hills Vineyard Inn. Which had been donated in an attempt to gain business via the Berdize sisters.

Conrad was the only person without so much as a boater hat. Jane didn't want to say he was a fuddy duddy in the dress-up department, but he was absolutely a fuddy duddy. Somehow, she dated him anyway. Adored him, really. Hmm. No, she wasn't comfortable using the A word to describe the man who'd kissed the breath from her lungs only weeks ago. At her invitation. A mistake she couldn't allow herself to make again. Not more than a few more times. Twenty, max. Maybe thirty. Possibly fifty. She...kinda liked him. Yes, a much better description.

Her phone buzzed again. Groaning, she checked the message.

C-Berdize: *Are the perp and vic not ready? Is that the problem???*

Perp? Vic? Apparently, Charlotte had listened to a few crime podcasts to get in the spirit of things.

Jane replied with a thumbs up emoji. Fiona was playing the cut-throat killer. Absolutely no one would suspect her. But where was Beau, the victim?

Great! Now Jane had two missing actors.

Beau was a vet who ran Peach State Security and oversaw the cemetery's daily protection. She admired and trusted him with every fiber of her being. The blond giant added spice to her life. As anyone with taste buds knew, spices made everything better.

Half an hour ago, he'd claimed he'd left something important at her onsite cottage. She'd asked him to check on her beloved cat, Rolex, the world's most perfect housepanther, while he was there. Then and now, Jane suspected Beau planned to hide out for a bit. He'd made it clear he despised the quote unquote *too tight* costume she'd chosen for his character, Clyde Talmadge. A bootlegger who'd obtained his gold the old-fashioned way—by stealing it from a bank.

Faithful Beau should have returned long ago. Unless Rolex had killed him. Or Beau had decided to perform a last-minute perimeter check with his crew, three other vets slash security experts. Two of them—Isaac and Holden—were supposed to walk the grounds, ensuring everyone played nice. The third, Trick, was checking tickets and IDs at the door, making sure no one entered the paid event without proof of purchase; he also kept track of everyone who so much as neared the gate. After finding two fresh corpses on the property earlier this year, Jane was taking no chances. Better to have a list of those in the vicinity. Just in case. No way trouble could find her tonight.

"Oh!" Fiona squealed, clasping Jane's wrist. "He's here, he's here!"

She knew that tone. Sheriff Moore must have arrived.

Scanning...Yep. Sure enough. She spotted the bald-headed, silver-bearded, barrel-chested grandfather striding their way. And oh, wow. He appeared exhausted, with deep lines of strain bracketing his eyes.

He stopped in front of Fiona and looked her over. "I'm sorry I'm late but— Lord, save me." He added nothing else, but then, he didn't need to. His awed tone said plenty.

All confidence and playfulness, Fiona fiddled with her string of pearls. "No need to worry, Sheriff. You were worth the wait."

He did look charming in his 1920s bathing costume. A big striped T-shirt with matching shorts and knee-high stockings. But goodness gracious. Someone cut this sexual tension with a chainsaw already.

"Flirt on your own time, guys." Jane gave Fiona a gentle nudge toward the Valley of the Dolls, the section set up for the pretend murder of the century. "Do you have your walkie-talkie?"

Fiona patted the device clipped to the back of her belt. "Sure do."

"Excellent. I have mine, as well." Jane lifted her beaded purse. "Now go. Find Beau and take your places. We gotta start."

"Miss me." Her friend blew Sheriff Moore a kiss, then sauntered away.

"Break a leg, Fee," he called, pulling at the shirt's rounded neckline.

Executing a full circle turn, she called back, "Darling, I'm going to break a whole lot more than Beau's leg, and that's a fact."

True, considering her character used a bag of gold to beat the thief to death. All in good fun, of course.

Jane withdrew a folded paper from her purse and thrust it into the sheriff's hands. "Step up to the microphone and read this." When he remained in place, one brow arched, she remembered her manners and added, "Please and thank you."

"That's better." He nodded and did as instructed. "Good evening, everyone, and welcome."

As conversations died down, Jane made her way off stage and veered toward the back exit. Tonight, she had the distinct honor of manning the information desk. People would have questions. People always had questions. Those fifty-dollar tickets bought answers.

"The time is the roaring twenties, when the gold mines of Aurelian Hills have all but petered out, forcing residents to move west." The sheriff's (normal) voice followed her into the cool, open air outside the tent. "But wait. In a stroke of good fortune, the notorious Clyde Talmadge finds one last rich vein in the Savings and..." The words faded.

Only seconds later, participants shot from the tent and

scattered in every direction. Even before Jane reached her table, people congregated around her.

"Where's the bathroom?"

"I've lost my map. Do you have an extra?'

"Can we have more than four people on a team?"

"Can we have *less* than four people on a team?"

Minutes passed like hours as she stopped to answer every query. Ugh! Her feet already throbbed. She hadn't planned on standing so long in these vintage 1920s heels.

"Where's the–" The speaker went quiet abruptly, his eyes widening.

A firm hand settled on Jane's hip, startling a gasp out of her. Then a husky voice full of authority and dreams proclaimed, "Ms. Ladling has nothing more to say until she reaches the designated information booth."

The fragrance of dry cedar and refined spice hit her senses, and she smiled, melting into her accoster. See! Spices made everything better.

Conrad kissed her temple as he escorted her away. "Thank you, sweetheart."

"You are more than welcome." Oh, how she loved–*liked, only liked,* when he called her sweetheart. "But, um." She chewed on her bottom lip. "Which of my wondrous deeds are you thanking me for?"

"Your honesty with Fiona... regarding my sizzling hot buttered buns."

Jane nearly swallowed her tongue, her cheeks flushing hotter than ever. "What—how—oh!" Realization slapped her upside the head. Eek! She'd forgotten that her phone acted as a constant listening device for the evening, feeding straight to earpieces worn by Conrad and Beau. By her request! But oh, the app broadcasting her conversations to the boys was supposed to keep her from being accused of murder a third time, not put all her tush-admiring on blast.

Like a true gentleman, Conrad held up the rope that cordoned off the area designated for volunteers and wait staff. She ducked inside, and he followed her through. Aww. He strode over to pull the chair at her table. Even sweeter!

"Thank you." Jane eased down. Hmm. She should have added a cushion, considering she'd be spending the next two hours sitting here. Or longer! Depended on the winner and how long it took them to unravel the (brilliant) mystery.

At least she had a gorgeous view of the reflection area—the perfect distraction from Conrad's tantalizing nearness. A magnificent wisteria tree stretched long branches over a circle of benches. Beyond them, a handful of shop owners had set up booths. Other stalls lined the cobblestone walkway leading toward every subdivision of the cemetery. All but the former business center, near where the "murder" took place. According to Grandma Lily, that one-story Victorian cottage once acted as the hub for Garden of Memories. Now ivy grew in abandon over the yellowing paint and caving roof.

One day, Jane hoped to raise enough money to restore the building to its original glory.

"Ignoring me won't do you any good. Me and my buns are still here." Conrad moved to the front of the table, flattened his palms on the surface and leaned down. When the heat cranked up in her cheeks, he grinned, revealing straight, white teeth. "Do I need to give you another reason not to fall for me?"

To help her avoid the curse, he enjoyed teasing her with "terrible" facts about himself. She should say no—those facts only made her adore—*like* him more. But the game was too fun to stop.

"Yes. Absolutely." She nodded with enthusiasm. "Make it the worst one yet, please."

"All right. Here goes." His amber eyes sparkled. "I don't care how toilet paper hangs."

She gasped. Actually, genuinely gasped. "Conrad! That's insanity. There is a correct way and a wrong way, and that is irrefutable."

His grin returned, only it was the lopsided one she found irresistible. "I better go. Do me a favor and try not to objectify me as I walk away."

"Yes. Well," she responded primly. "I can't make any promises on that score."

He snorted, then reached out to ghost his knuckles along the curve of her jaw. Her lips parted at the first brush of contact, and her breath hitched. His amusement evaporated, revealing something achingly tender.

Uh-oh. They were having a moment, weren't they?

Lingering, he searched her gaze with his own. The rest of the world vanished, and she gulped. *I do not love him. I don't. I won't.* Getting her heart broken when things fell apart was one thing. Letting someone break her darling Rolex's heart was quite another. What if her perfect little feline came to depend on Conrad, then boom, the special agent was gone?

"I want to take you on a date tomorrow night," he intoned.

The moisture in her mouth dried. "A *date* date? As in, just the two of us?" Instead of sharing a meal at her place with the rest of the gang? AKA Fiona, Beau, his pals, and the sheriff. Team Truth, Jane liked to call them.

"Yes. A *date* date. Just the two of us. Think about it. Then say yes out loud." Eyes twinkling again, he tapped his ear, reminding her that he would be listening. "I'll come by and check on you in about an hour. We can discuss restaurants." With that, he walked off, leaving her alone with her thoughts. And a bout of panic.

Not that she planned to indulge either one. Or think

about dating. The people who'd stood off to the side, waiting for his departure, swarmed her. She answered question after question with few pauses. Time evaporated. She knew this for a fact because anytime she glanced at the clock, at least ten minutes had passed in a matter of seconds.

Exactly one hour later, Conrad returned as promised. The crowd parted like the Red Sea.

"I haven't used the word yes even once," she rushed out.

"Not true. You just did." His eyes were twinkling again. "So, where would you like to eat?"

"I—" A blood-curdling scream suddenly pierced the night, and every cell in Jane's body vibrated with alarm.

She groaned. Trouble had just found her, it seemed.

CHAPTER TWO

"If you're not lying, you're not trying."
Anthony "Tony" Miller, attorney at law

In a thundering flap of wings, birds took flight from multiple trees. Around Jane, conversations ceased, and people went still. The only movement came from flashing lightning bugs.

Acid pooled in her stomach. That hadn't been a startled, playful, or victorious sound. No, terror had filled every nuance. "What in the world?" She jumped to her feet, the fringe on her dress tapping against her knees.

Guests started laughing. A few even clapped and cheered.

They thought the scream was part of the event?

A line formed between Conrad's eyes. He strode around the table to stand beside her. "I read your script, but I don't recall an impromptu shriek."

"I know." Jane tightened her grip on the pen she held. "I think something's wrong." There hadn't been a second scream, at least. That was a good sign, right?

The corners of his mouth turned down. "I'm sure Beau

and his guys are on it. But, considering the murderous nature of the townsfolk, I better go check it out."

Her breath released in a rush, and she kissed his cheek. "Yes, please, and thank you."

"For you, anything. Stay here. Please." Expression intent, he lightly pinched her chin, angled her face the way he wanted it, and kissed her mouth. An action she hadn't known she'd needed until just then.

As he pivoted and stalked off, her hand fluttered to her throat. Returning to the seat, she muttered, "No reason to panic." For all she knew, someone had solved the case super early, discovered Beau's body, and witnessed Fiona absconding with a stolen bag of fake gold. Yes, yes, that must be what happened.

A crackling sound rose from Jane's purse. Confused, she dug inside–duh! The walkie-talkie. Beau had insisted all cast members carry a two-way radio in case of an emergency.

Heart thumping, she lifted the device to her mouth. "Yes. Hello?"

"Jane!" Fiona whisper-yelled, the words drenched in horror. "Jane, there's been a murder. A real one! There's blood. And a needle!"

Blood? Needle? "What?!" This could *not* be happening. Not again. Not on this special night of celebration and fun. She'd taken every precaution.

"I'm so sorry," her friend rushed on. "I shouldn't have left the Valley of the Dolls, but Beau never showed up. I went looking for him and...and...that's when I found it." Her volume dropped to a whisper without the yell. "The body. He's one hundred percent dead, Jane. I checked for a pulse. You're the expert in such matters. What am I supposed to do now?"

Wait, wait, wait. "Who's dead?" Not Beau. Please, please not Beau.

The mayor approached the information table, saying, "Can you tell me where–"

"I'm on my way," she told Fiona, ignoring him. Stay put? No. As the mayor sputtered, Jane shot to her feet. With only the walkie talkie in hand, she dashed through the cemetery, taking the same path as Conrad, her high heels clacking on the cobblestone walkway. After stumbling twice, she kicked off her shoes, uncaring when little rocks dug into her soles. "Fee? Are you there? Where are you?"

"I'm close to the original office." Crackling. "I don't want to leave his body."

"Whose body?" she demanded.

"Oh! I figured out what to do. I'm calling Sheriff Moore." *Click.*

Argh! Surely *Jane* wasn't so annoying when she stumbled upon a corpse.

Adjusting her route, she pumped her arms to pick up speed. She flew past the statue of Muffin, the cemetery's canine guardian, then zigged and zagged between residents, all while doing her best to avoid party goers still searching for clues.

"Sorry!" she rushed out anytime she grazed someone.

When she crossed into Eden Valley, the crowd vanished. From there, she hurried past the mausoleum and entered Paradise Ladling, an area filled with her relatives. To discourage visitors in this particular section, she'd temporarily shut off the lights along the pathway. It helped that towering trees covered in Spanish moss blocked the moonlight.

With a fresh burst of energy, Jane crested a slope.

"Whoa. Slow down there, girl," commanded a voice from the shadows.

With a jolt, she skidded to a halt. Who the heck– "Oh!

Sheriff Moore." She pressed a palm over her racing heart as he stepped forward. "What are you doing, skulking about?"

"I wasn't skulking. I dropped my phone, which doubled as my flashlight. But the light switched off upon impact. Considering it's pitch black out here and I can't navigate the winding hedgerows by memory, I decided to wait for you. I knew you'd come along sooner or later." He tapped his temple. "That's called using my resources."

"Hang on." Having left her own phone behind, she jogged to a nearby gardenia bush without flowers. Small wooden chests with flashlights were hidden in every section of the Garden. A just-in-case practice started by Grandma Lily and continued by Jane, though she'd progressed from bulbs to LEDs. There should be a chest right…here.

The ancient lid lifted with a groan, and she reached inside. Tada! With a flick of her thumb, they had light. Thankfully, it didn't take long to locate his phone.

"I also use my resources wisely," she said, handing over his property.

As they moved forward, he made a quick call to a deputy, requesting backup. Despite the evening chill, sweat glistened on his concern-etched face. "What did Fee tell you?" he demanded as soon as he hung up. "I spoke to her only minutes ago, but couldn't get much out of her."

"Only that she'd found a man's body in this area. But I don't see her anywhere nearby. Or the body. Do you?"

"Nope," he said, huffing and puffing.

Well. "She must be somewhere behind the big tree." Jane held her breath as they rounded the massive hickory in question. What was she soon to find? "Did she tell you who died?"

"Negative."

Her stomach curdled. *Who, who?* Desperate for answers, Jane continued forward, scanning the darkness until she found a swath of light. Approaching an overgrown crape myrtle, voices reached her ears. Through a tangle of branches, she finally spotted her friend, leaning against another oak, holding a lantern.

Conrad knelt beside the body, using his phone as a flashlight. Oh, thank goodness! There was Beau, off to the side, whispering with his three coworkers. He hadn't perished on her ancestral estate.

"All right. I need everyone to step back," Conrad called as he straightened. "Now." He stretched out his arms, prompting the group to obey. He'd gone into full GBH mode.

Sheriff Moore beelined straight to Fiona, who made a beeline for him, too. "Fee!"

"Oh, Raymond," Fiona cried, burrowing into his big frame. "The night wasn't supposed to end this way."

Needing a little comforting of her own, Jane launched herself at Conrad. He didn't wave her off but caught her, wrapping his strong arms around her waist, holding her steady. She'd reached her safe place. Which meant…

Time to focus. She had another mystery to solve.

Jane noted the victim's features. Thick dark hair streaked with gray. The beginnings of an unkempt beard. Thin and wiry frame, like a caged animal. His identity clicked. This was none other than Tony Miller. Her onetime lawyer and two-time murder suspect.

Tony lay on his side, one cheek resting upon a small puddle of blood. A smear of crimson wet the other cheek. His open eyes stared at nothing. Patches of his skin possessed a purplish, grayish tint. His dark, three-piece suit was wrinkled, but not torn. A couple feet away rested a fallen fedora hat.

"What happened?" she asked with a slight tremor.

Conrad kissed her temple. "I'll let the others explain. I've got to make a call."

"Yes, of course." Justice for Tony came first. She understood. After giving the agent a reassuring squeeze, she stepped aside.

Conrad told the sheriff, "Considering I'm on the scene and GBH has handled the last two murders in Aurelian Hills, I'm taking the lead on this. Keep Jane, Fiona, and Beau with you. Do you have deputies who can block the guests from this area and corral everyone in the tent? No one leaves without permission."

"I've called for reinforcements, and they should arrive any minute," Sheriff Moore said. "Until then, we can send Beau's team to do the blocking and corralling."

Conrad nodded, then made his call.

A man assured of his authority, the sheriff motioned to Beau. "You heard him, son. Over here with me." To Isaac, Holden and Trick, he barked orders, sending the threesome flying in opposite directions. Through it all, he maintained his hold on Fiona.

Jane walked over, kissed her friend's cheek, then hugged Beau. "I was so afraid it was you."

He pulled back and gave her shoulder a reassuring pat. "I'm pretty tough to kill."

Conrad spoke into his phone, "No ma'am, I do not enjoy disturbing you on your night off. But there's been another death at Garden of Memories in Aurelian Hills. Probable homicide." A pause. He scowled, his gaze cutting to Jane for a moment. "Hard to say until we learn time of death." Pause. "No ma'am, half the town surrounded her." Pause. "Yes ma'am. Give the case to Hightower if you want. I understand."

Great. Jane was a suspect right off the bat. But okay. No big deal. She just needed to figure out what the heck happened. Conrad had said probable homicide. What made him discount, say, an accidental drug overdose? Hadn't Fiona mentioned a needle? Tony could've fallen and hit his head on a rock.

Determined to collect photographic evidence to study later, Jane traded her flashlight for Beau's phone. And the dear man let her. "Keep the light as close to the body as you can."

The second her friend complied, she snapped as many crime scene photos as possible, as stealthily as possible. No need to trouble Conrad by asking for permission...and doing it anyway after he told her no.

"The killer made doubly sure Tony died," Beau explained quietly. "He—or she—hit him in the head with a bag of our gold at least three times. His body also shows signs of a drug overdose. Fiona plucked a syringe out of his neck when she found him. She dropped it in the grass, near the hat."

Icy cold crept down Jane's spine. "She's a suspect, isn't she?"

"For sure. But so am I. The gold is the one I misplaced earlier." He pointed to a spot close to Tony's feet, where a small brown bag Jane had sewn only days ago now featured brand new bloodstains.

She took a handful of additional photos and returned the phone to Beau. "Text me those images right away. And don't worry. Team Truth will figure this out." Fiona and Beau weren't guilty. But someone was.

Conrad ended his call, heaved a weary sigh, then joined the group. Drawn like a magnet to metal, Jane eased into him. He welcomed her nearness, slinging an arm around her waist once again.

"My men are here," Sheriff Moore announced, ending a call of his own. "Holden is helping them usher the participants into the tent. Soon as that's done, they'll take statements."

"I'll need a list of guests," Conrad told Jane before casting a grim look at Fiona. "And a detailed account of your whereabouts once you left the welcome tent."

Uh oh. Did *Conrad* think the darling grandmother was capable of murder? Because that would be an immediate relationship ender.

Fiona closed her fingers in the sheriff's shirt, clinging to him. "I'm happy to explain my whereabouts...after I speak with my lawyer. Which I'll do right away. Just as soon as I hire him." She looked to the sheriff, who nodded encouragingly. Had he told her what to say? "There's one here at the party. I'll find him in the crowd."

Ugh. How had things dovetailed so quickly?

"As for you." The special agent gave Jane a little squeeze. "Sheriff Moore will escort you, Fiona and Beau to the tent. Since you're going to take more photos with or without my permission, be sure to get me candid shots of the guests, without being as obvious as you were with Mr. Miller."

Did the special agent miss nothing?

Jane saluted him. "Don't worry, everyone," she said, only then realizing she, too, clutched a man's shirt. "Everything's gonna be all right. I'm on the case."

THE NIGHT SEEMED to last both an eternity and a blip. GBH agents arrived by the droves, tromping through Jane's immaculate cemetery for the third time in four months, treating the shrubbery as if it had committed the murder. Did no one mind their manners anymore?

"This is the best murder mystery party ever!" someone called.

Others laughingly agreed.

Jane made her way through the tent, secretly

photographing everyone as requested. The Berdize sisters noticed and posed, giving her a thumbs up. No doubt their company would be mentioned in every upcoming news report, tweet and post. They'd be hailed as the most authentic party planners in history. New commissions would roll in.

"This is serious business, people, not a game," a woman exclaimed. Agent Karen Hightower, Jane's least favorite investigator of all time. During the last case, the no-nonsense dictator with an inverted bob had hoped to lock her in prison and throw away the key. "Someone died."

Several people bowed their head in shame, including the Berdize sisters. Others acted as if the agent participated in the game and saluted her.

At the moment, Hightower was questioning Beau, Fiona, and Fiona's attorney—an older gent who reminded Jane of Al Capone. The foursome had been in conversation for over an hour. Her gut shouted, *That can't be good.*

Had she mentioned the agent was her least favorite investigator ever?

Finally, the group broke apart. Beau approached Jane, his expression grim. Fiona followed him with tight lips and a brave face.

"We've been cleared to leave while the authorities finish up." Beau massaged the back of his neck. "Let's head to your cottage."

Jane scanned the crowd, hoping to catch a final glance of Conrad. He'd come in and out of the tent multiple times. No sign of him. Disappointment surged.

With a bump of his shoulder, Beau nudged her toward the exit. "Last time your Agent Spice was here, he asked me to make sure you got home safely."

Well. Warmth filled her chest, drowning the disappointment. Again and again that man showed how much he cared for her. It made her all fluttery and—Whoa! *What are you doing? Taunting the curse?* "Thank you. I'm grateful for your escort."

They trudged through the grounds in silence, each lost in thought. On the cottage porch, Beau paused long enough to speak in hushed whispers with his friends, who were there waiting. The trio nodded at her before stalking to their vehicles, their booted feet crunching on gravel.

"Are Holden, Trick and Isaac coming back?" Jane asked.

"No," Beau replied. "They'll study the Garden's security feed while the feds organize a warrant."

Ugh. Did she hold the record for the most warrants issued in the shortest amount of time?

"Good plan. This is the perfect time to compare notes and figure out what I'm going to tell my kids," Fiona said, her strain obvious. "If I'm telling them anything, that is. I don't want my precious grandbabies thinking Nana FeeFee is a criminal. Oh! Where are my manners? Is anyone hungry? Why don't I make us a light midnight snack?" She bolted to the kitchen the moment they got inside.

The precious woman puttered around, whipping up waffle BLTs and fried cheese stuffed Doritos. Jane joined Beau at the counter, perched atop a barstool, and watched. Fiona had been part of her life since, well, always. So much so, the grandmother seemed to be one with the décor. From the harvest gold appliances and dark wood paneling to Grandma Lily's love of decoupaging with mushrooms.

"Tell us everything that happened and leave nothing out," Jane said as Rolex jumped into her lap. She kissed his handsome face and scratched behind his adorable ears. He hissed at Beau.

In front of the stove, Fiona poured batter into a waffle iron. "I'm happy to start. Just as soon as Beau tells us where he was all night."

The vet slinked in his seat, earning another hiss from Rolex. Plus a swipe of the claws.

Jane gave her baby another kiss and cooed her praise. "Such a good guard cat."

For a split second, her friend looked ready to smile. And oh, wow, he was gorgeous when he almost smiled. And when he actually smiled. And even when he didn't. He had tons of muscles, wavy blond hair, and green eyes. Although, those eyes tended to veer toward somber most times, the seriousness of his gaze reminding Jane of his past trials. Having returned from several tours of duty overseas, Beau dealt with his fair share of mental horrors. At least, she assumed. He hadn't shared much.

"And you," she told her friend, patting his hand. "Such a dapper gentleman." He still wore the roaring twenties costume Jane selected for him. A glorious ensemble, complete with red and white striped jacket, a satin bow tie, and a braided straw boater hat with a red-ribboned band. Was it a little too tight? Yes. But that only made it better.

He wrinkled his nose at her. "The highlight of my day will be tearing off this eyesore."

"Well, I never." Jane's back straightened with mock affront. "I'll have you know that outfit was chosen with care. A way to help you stand out."

"I look like I should be singing a four-part harmony in a barbershop quartet."

Fiona smothered a laugh. Good. Considering the heaviness of the evening, a touch of levity was good for everyone.

"I'll be honest with you." He shrugged out of the jacket. "I'm not ready to discuss my whereabouts with you. I've spoken to Conrad, and one day soon, I'll tell you too. Until then... Just know I wasn't doing anything wrong."

Jane rolled her eyes. "We never thought you did anything wrong." He was one of the most honorable guys she'd ever met. Someone who deserved the love and comfort of an equally honorable woman.

Twice she'd tried to set him up on dates with former classmates. The first had never returned her calls, and the other had died on her front porch last month. Perhaps Jane should start a new search? But dang it. Curiosity had never been her friend. What was Beau hiding? And did he not understand she could only handle one mystery at a time?

She opened her mouth to ask a follow up question, but he swiveled in his chair and focused on Fiona. "Weren't you going to tell us what led to your discovery of the body?"

Jane took the bait, flowing with the change of subject. "And in the Valley of Dolls, no less." Not the location of the fake murder. No, oh, no. That would be too easy. There were no cameras in the Valley. Not that she intended to remind her friends of the lack, considering she insisted on leaving the area as is.

Due to a shortage of funds, she'd refused Beau's offer to add equipment out there, assuming a single plot of land could never become the stage for two different crimes. Had she shown the slightest interest in agreement, he would've spent his own money to do it. Again! That, she couldn't allow. Or so she'd thought. Her inability to receive a gift from a dear friend had just come with a hefty price tag.

"You weren't checking in, Beau, and the clock was ticking." Fiona finished off a waffle and poured batter for the next. "I figured I should search for you before anyone guessed the location of your murder. I hadn't realized how far I'd walked until I heard a man cursing. I creeped closer, thinking a guest had snuck over to dig up a grave, on the hunt for genuine gold. I'm sure everyone remembers when we dealt with *that*."

"I certainly do," Jane exploded with a nod. Her exuberance startled Rolex. The world's most flawless feline hopped from her lap to the table and curled up in his favorite spot—the centerpiece bowl. He closed his eyes, instantly asleep and so cute he should be a catalog model. "But no gravedigger is a match for Team Truth. We stop bad guys but good!"

Fiona nodded, flipping the waffle iron. "So true. Well. By the time I reached Tony, he was already dead and whoever killed him was gone. I'm guessing the culprit had only just run off. I'm pretty sure I heard a patter of footsteps."

"Beau told me Tony was beaten, too." Hmm. Tony had an ex-wife. Emma Miller, a local nurse Jane had accused of murder. Someone who had a fiery temper *and* access to drugs. Though Emma hadn't committed the first or second homicide, she definitely probably could have committed this one.

And a woman scorned certainly fit the narrative. According to Conrad, murders usually occurred for one of two reasons: love or money. The couple had only recently split up due to Emma's affair with a philandering doctor, the first victim. Maybe the exes had fought over bills, property, or even custody of their dog, Cheddar.

For the record, murder could be an option if anyone attempted to steal Rolex from Jane.

"Am I going to jail, Beau?" Fiona asked without facing him, the slightest quiver in her voice.

Jane clutched her stomach to ward off a sudden ache. How she hated seeing her friend in such a worried state.

"I promise you, you are not," he said. "I looked into Tony after Jane hired him. He wasn't a well liked guy. We might be suspects now, but there will be many others, I assure you."

"How about this?" She purposely added a note of brightness to her tone. "As Fiona finishes preparing tonight's nibbles, we'll compare everything we saw Tony do, everyone we noticed speaking with him, and every location we know he visited. If we aren't too tired, we can watch the security feed afterward. We might notice something the three hotties miss."

Beau snorted. "Three hotties? Please never call them that again."

"You're right," she said with a nod. "A better description is triple stack snack cake."

He leaned closer to tweak her nose. "You do know that you are ridiculous, yes?"

"I do." Conrad told her often. She batted her lashes at her friend. "But I'm always lovable."

"You two stop being so cute with each other and grab some plates." Fiona shredded a block of cheese. "I'm ready to get to comparing."

"This is going to be another all-nighter, isn't it?" Beau checked his phone, pursed his lips, then stood and strode to the proper cabinet.

Jane's brain immediately started rolling, of course. "Do you have a midnight appointment?" She propped her elbows on the counter. "Please, share with the rest of the class."

"How has Conrad not tanned your hide yet?" He handed her a plate before opening the correct drawer to fish out forks. "I'm staying, okay? I'm helping. We'll figure this out."

Yes, they would. Allowing her friends—her family!—to be blamed for a murder they didn't commit wasn't happening. Not on Jane's watch. She wasn't even sure she'd let them be blamed for a murder they *did* commit.

"All right. Here's my accounting," Fiona said, battering a chip in different bowls before dropping it into boiling oil. "Before I headed to the Valley of the Dolls, I spotted Tony guzzling alcohol from a flask."

"I saw him drinking too!" Jane exclaimed.

Fiona nodded. "He stood in a corner, in the shadows of the biggest balloon arch, glaring at someone or something."

"Yes. Exactly."

"About ten minutes after the crowd flooded the cemetery," Beau piped up, "I saw him with Devin Hagger. The two were whispering, and the posture of both suggested those whispers weren't friendly."

"Hagger is my attorney," the older woman said, chewing on her bottom lip. "He and Tony were partners. Raymond thought that might work in my favor, but now I'm wondering..."

First, it was good to know Beau had been on cemetery grounds while in the midst of his mysterious disappearance. Second, who or what had Tony glared at? Maybe later Jane would make a diorama of the tent to figure out his sightline–and the most likely candidate. Third, she wondered about Hagger too. Had the partners disliked each other?

"Tony didn't get along with anyone, it seemed," she said. "I also saw him near the help's table twice. The first time, he was alone. He strode past me, tossing me his customary scowl." They hadn't exactly parted on the best of terms. "The second time, he stopped at the Bank of Aurelian Hills booth to chat with Lucy Chang. I couldn't make out their words, not that I tried to, but their body language spoke volumes. They weren't discussing the merits of opening a savings account, that's for sure."

Fiona passed out food, and they dug in. Amazing flavors deluged Jane. The conversation continued, but no new revelations came to light. By the time they finished washing the dishes, they were too blurry eyed to study the security feed, so they said their goodbyes.

Planning to sleep for two years—minimum—Jane changed into her pajamas and crawled into bed. Rolex snuggled into her side, not budging when she tossed and turned, unable to sleep for some reason. Finally she gave up and grabbed her phone. Why not bug Conrad?

A yawn cracked her jaw as she texted the special agent.

Since I know you're curious, my top two suspects are Emma Miller and Lucy Chang. For reasons. But also Devin Hagger.

In fact, Jane planned to have a chat with both women tomorrow. Any interaction with Hagger would have to be scheduled, she was sure.

The darling man's reply came within seconds. **Agent Spice**: *Sweetheart, I'm ten steps ahead of you. Check your purse.*

Wait. What? Beyond curious, Jane scrambled out of bed and rooted around her cluttered bedroom to find the purse she'd slung… there! She dumped out the contents, riffled through everything and discovered a small piece of paper she didn't recognize.

In bold black ink were the words *You suspect Emma Miller, Lucy Chang & Devin Hagger.*

How had–when had–gah! When she flipped the page over, she discovered another message. PS *Stop falling for me. I snore.*

A smile bloomed as she clutched the paper to her chest. Oh, how she lo–*liked* that man. Liked. Definitely only liked.

Shaking now, Jane gulped and climbed back into bed. Once again, she tossed and turned. This time, however, she did it for an entirely different reason.

CHAPTER THREE

"Winning isn't everything—is something losers say."
Emma Miller, nurse

A frantic knock roused Jane from a deep sleep. What the heck? Had Beau returned and begun some kind of repair on the house? Yeah, probably. The generous muscle man was always doing things like that.

Rolex sprang from the bed, juddering the mattress as Jane sat up. She blinked repeatedly, trying to clear her vision. To think. Details hit her, one after the other. Cottage. Bedroom. Clutter. Hats everywhere.

She snatched up her phone to check the time. 11:06 a.m. Oh, dang. Usually she was up by five sharp and on the grounds an hour later to open the gate and begin her morning walk about, making lists of any plots in need of tending, then doing the actual tending. The Garden was her home. Her sanctuary. A place of beauty and serenity.

A notification on the cell's screen caught her eye, and her pulse jumped. Seven texts awaited her. Meaning, seven more than usual. Two from the Berdize sisters, letting her know the party had been a raging success, and they'd love to put another event on the books. Two came from a reporter at The Headliner—a town message board app as well as a new weekly paper. The woman hoped to interview Jane for a story about Tony's murder.

A stranger left an irate text demanding a refund. How had they discovered her private number, anyway?

Beau sent one, informing her that he'd watched the security footage, found nothing helpful or hurtful yet, but the warrant had come through, and he'd handed over the feed.

The last message came from Conrad.

Agent Spice: *GBH will be all over the cemetery again today. We've cordoned off certain areas you'll need to avoid. I'll stop by the cottage this evening for—I'm sure—a Jane Ladling interrogation. What we do afterward is up to you.*

Such an informative yet charming text. Dang him! Speaking of his terrible, wonderful charm. Was he *trying* to make her catch feelings?

Maybe agreeing to go on a first date had been a mistake. Big. Huge. She almost texted Fiona for advice. No doubt her friend was sleeping off a bad night, too. Better to wait. Besides, Jane should have a concrete lead on the case before she reached out.

Hey! Beau hadn't sent her those photos of the body. She'd just shoot him a quick text to–

The knocking started up again, and she groaned. Not caused by a hammer, after all, but a fist. Someone persistent pounded at the front door, desperate to get her attention.

She set her phone aside, threw her legs over the mattress, and stood, giving herself a full body scan. She wore a T-shirt that read "My Cat is Better Than Your Cat" and a pair of ruffled pink pants. Not bad, but not great, either. Oh, well. Uninvited guests got what they got.

The door whacking came faster and harder.

"I'm coming," she called, grabbing and donning a fluffy white robe covered with black cats. She padded to the front door and checked the peephole.

Rolex was already there, waiting, eager to hiss and claw at the intruder.

Her jaw went slack. What the—*what?* Emma Miller, here in the flesh. But, but...Jane had expected to corner the nurse at the clinic. In town. Why would a top suspect hunt *her* down?

Trembling, she flipped the lock and twisted the knob to reveal the nurse, who wore scrubs and projected all kinds of upset. She held a leash, with a red and white corgi at the end of it. The infamous Cheddar. The little cutie grinned and wagged his docked tail, as happy as could be.

"Oh, good. You're awake," Emma said, seeming relieved and nervous at once. Had she stopped by on her lunch break or something?

"Um...Hi?" Jane didn't know the woman well. To be honest, they'd only interacted a few times. And each of those times had involved a murder case.

"Hi." The other woman opened and closed her mouth, as if searching for her next words. She was a pretty, with thickly lashed eyes and honey-colored hair too dark to be blond, but too light to be brown. Red rimmed her eyes, as if she'd been crying.

Rolex prowled onto the porch with panther-like stealth, closing in on Cheddar. The dog leaned down to sniff the feline's head. Her kitty reared back with a hiss. Fast as a bullet, he darted into the house while Cheddar whined. How adorable. She'd have to pull a clip from the security feed and create a loop of the interaction. Then she could watch it again and again on repeat.

Cheeks paler by the second, the nurse finally settled on, "May I come in?"

A thousand thoughts raced through Jane's mind. Was *she* soon to be accused of murder? Verbally attacked? Questioned? What, what?

Curiosity was getting the better of her. Too many mysteries in the past two days. Why not solve this one? But. If she welcomed a murder suspect inside the cottage, Conrad would protest. But. He himself hadn't declared a suspect yet. So. Technically, Emma wasn't really a suspect to anyone but Jane. When she factored in the amount of information that could be gleaned from a single conversation, well, turning the woman away seemed like the far more foolish option.

"Please," she said, using her sweetest tone. She pivoted and waved an arm. "Do come in."

Emma and Cheddar entered the cottage, the dog's nails clacking on the hardwood floor. Both mother and pet examined the small living room. Jane did the same, trying to see everything as they must. Hmm. Maybe it was time to buy a slipcover for the orange velvet couch. Even with the beautiful, handmade throw tossed over the back, Grandma Lily's sofa had seen better days. No way Jane could let it go.

Years ago, her Pops used to stretch across the cushions and work his favorite puzzles. Word scrambles, crosswords, you name it. And Grandma Lily had perched right there on the center cushion and asked if young Jane would like to stay at the Garden rather than live with her mom. That couch had even supported her as she'd read her first Regency romance novel, featuring Victorian maidens and dashing dukes.

"You have a lovely home," the nurse muttered, interrupting Jane's parade of memories.

"Thank you." Scratch out accused of murder and verbally attacked. "Um. Have a seat while I make coffee." She didn't wait for a response, but hightailed it into the kitchen.

As she shuffled about, filling the pot and spooning pumpkin spice coffee grounds into the appropriate location

—because, yes, she was one of *those* people—she planned the upcoming interrogation.

Okay. So. She should probably be direct. To the point. Blunt, even. Fiona and Beau counted on her. Conrad, too, though he most likely didn't know it and absolutely wouldn't admit it. Honestly, the poor thing didn't have a creative bone in his scrumptious body. No, he was all logic and facts.

As morning's most amazing scent filled the room, Jane breathed deep. She poured two mugs, added a healthy dose of cream and sugar because no one in their right mind drank it plain, then returned to the living area. If Emma protested the sweetness, well, she had definitely killed her ex-husband.

The other woman perched on the couch. Despite being bound by the leash, Cheddar trotted around the well-loved coffee table, sniffing every inch. Where was—ah. Rolex lay beneath the table, cool as a cucumber and glaring daggers at the dog, daring him to make a move. Too. Adorable.

Jane handed over a mug and dashed out of toss-a-hot-beverage-in-her-face range just in case. She settled in a chair across from her visitor, who hadn't calmed much. "So. How may I help you?" she asked. Good. Direct and to the point, as planned.

"I'd like to hire you to find Tony's killer," Emma rushed out, as if the words had been poised at the edge of her tongue for far too long.

"Um. Excuse me?" Jane blinked and shook her head. Surely she'd misheard. "Can you repeat that?"

Her guest placed the mug on the coffee table, politely using a coaster despite the many nicks and scratches that decorated the surface. Without tasting the beverage. Why? Who didn't guzzle coffee by the gallon at every opportunity? "Look, I know we aren't friends. I also know the spouse—or ex-spouse in my case—is usually suspect number one in a situation like this." A humorless laugh escaped her. "GBH certainly thinks so. A few hours ago, two agents came by the clinic to ask about my access to opioids. Which I do not have! Before that, a new reporter at the Headliner called and questioned me about my divorce."

Opioids huh? Good to know the type of drug used. She sipped her own beverage, letting silence grow between them.

The nurse cracked, as hoped, and kept spewing facts. "They made me repeat my statement from last night to double check the details. Do you know what this means? They think I did it!"

"Well. Did you?"

"No! I swear I'm innocent. I didn't like Tony, but I wouldn't…I couldn't." Tears welled as Emma twisted the end of Cheddar's leash between her fingers. "Why would I hurt him? Our divorce was finalized. I'd moved on."

Maybe. But maybe not. Emma wasn't known for her honesty. During the first investigation, she'd lied about having an affair with the murdered doctor. The very cause of her divorce from Tony. Also the reason she'd gotten into a fistfight with the victim's widow. A dishonest disposition coupled with such a fiery temper might have led her to seek revenge against her husband for daring to leave her.

"Can you think of anyone else who might have wanted to harm Tony?" Jane asked.

"Are you kidding? Everyone in Aurelian Hills daydreamed about harming him." The tears streamed down the nurse's cheeks. "What if I'm being framed? What if Tony's killer took notes from Jake Stephenson, the last murderer to invade this town? I mean, Jake framed you and almost got away with his crime. What if I've been set up, too?"

Hmm. Another frame job? Seemed mighty convenient. Honestly, if Jane ever snapped and killed one of her enemies, she might pretend to be framed and hire someone to search for the culprit, too. What better way to involve yourself in the hunt to deflect suspicion?

On the other hand, she had indeed experienced the horrors of being accused of a crime she hadn't committed. Emma might be on to something.

On the other, other hand, Jane's original suspicions remained valid. Turning on the waterworks? A classic move of the guilty.

"I'll pay you whatever you want." Emma shifted in her seat. "Name your price."

Did the nurse have the kind of money needed to properly toss around phrases like "name your price?" Rumors suggested Tony had stiffed her hard in the settlement. Another reason for murder.

"More than my reputation is on the line." The other woman swiped at her damp cheeks with a trembling hand. "If I'm sent to prison, what will happen to my precious Cheddar?"

Oh man. Talk about a dagger to the heart. Also the most perfect thing to say to a fur mom as passionate as Jane. Too perfect? "Why not hire an experienced private detective?" Although, yes, she *had* considered opening her own agency for extra cash and adventure. Only one slight problem. She didn't quite fit the qualifications necessary for the great state of Georgia. Two years of experience with a licensed PI agency or a four-year degree in criminal justice.

"I admit I looked into it," Emma said, wringing her hands, "but the closest private detective lives in Atlanta. There's no way I'm paying a city boy—a stranger!—to poke around and bug the good people of Aurelian Hills. Who would even open up to him? Besides, you've more than proven your capabilities. You solved two cases already."

Jane's chin lifted. Yes, she had. Something GBH hadn't given her credit for, by the way.

Wait, was Emma attempting to butter her up?

"Please say yes, Jane. You've been in my shoes, so you understand. And you'll be investigating the case, anyway, right? I mean, I know agents spoke with Fiona and Beau at length." A sharp edge entered her tone. "Rumors are already circulating about their involvement."

Hold up. Did *Emma* think Fiona and Beau were guilty? Was this a fact-finding mission about two of the most wonderful people in existence? Well, how dare she!

Jane's grip on the mug tightened. Anyone who suspected the loving, beloved grandmother of three and the heroic war veteran with a heart of gold lacked common sense, and that was a fact.

Perhaps Emma hoped to shift blame onto someone—anyone—else. A far more likely scenario.

"If you think my friends are guilty," Jane grated, "why hire me? Aren't you afraid I'll help frame you to clear their names?"

"I did consider the possibility," Emma admitted. "Then I discarded it and decided to trust you. You're scarily honest and somehow a good judge of character." She drew in a deep breath and slowly exhaled. "Look. I doubt anyone else will take this case as seriously as you. Please," she repeated. "If not for me, do it for Cheddar."

Manipulation now? *Well played, Miller.* "Fine. I'll do it," she said and took another sip of her coffee. Clearly, Jane needed to keep a close watch on the nurse. "All I want in return is answers. And expenses." Just in case she incurred any unavoidable fees. "Perhaps a play date for our babies, too."

"Really? Oh, thank you, thank you, a thousand times, thank you," Emma cried. Cheddar forgot all about Rolex and jumped onto his mother's lap to lick her face. "See how happy you've made my little sweetie?"

Yes. Well. Maybe Emma was innocent, after all. Surely a

dog wouldn't love an evil murderess this intently. "Tell me everything that happened last night."

Nodding, eager, Emma wrapped her arms around her pet. "I attended your party, as I said, because I felt I deserved an evening of fun. With the divorce and Mark—Dr. Hotchkins, well, things have been…not fun lately."

Dr. Hotchkins, aka Dr. Hots. The first murder victim and the reason Jane met Special Agent Conrad Ryan. *Do* not *smile dreamily right now, Jay Bird.* Too late.

Emma's brow wrinkled with confusion. Still, she continued. "Tony was obviously trashed before he arrived. He was sneering, slurring his words, and insulting everyone who crossed his path. Especially me. He demanded to know if I had a boyfriend."

Ohhh. Good question. "Do you?"

"I've been on a few dates. Nothing serious, though." She shrugged, as if no big deal. "After several Mr. Wrongs, surely I'm due to find my Mr. Right." Despite her show of indifference, defensiveness had coated every word.

Hmm. A bit too cagey about her romantic interests? Not that Jane could blame her. When anyone asked her about Conrad, she tended to babble about everything and nothing at the same time.

"Tell me the name of every date." What if a would-be boyfriend had killed Tony in an attempt to impress Emma? Or out of jealousy. Or even to strike at her for being emotionally unavailable.

"Sure. I'm happy to text you a list. Not that it's long or anything," the nurse added in a rush. "But I met several guys online, and we chatted without going out."

"Anything else you remember about that night?"

"Well. Just that before the game started, I saw Tony arguing with Devin Hagger. His business partner."

Jane perked up. Beau had seen Devin Hagger, too. Last

night's suspicions resurged and solidified. What if the argument between partners had carried on, finally ending in murder? What if Hagger had agreed to help Fiona simply to make her look guiltier?

"I'm sorry. I don't know much more than that." Emma screwed up her nose, tears filling her eyes once again. "I had no idea my freedom would depend on keeping track of my ex-husband."

Been there. "You've given me enough to start." After she texted Fiona and suggested new representation, she'd consider telling Conrad everything she'd learned today, then speak with Lucy Chang and make an appointment with Devin Hagger. Initial consultations were usually free, right?

The nurse dug inside her purse with a shaky hand, withdrew her phone, and requested Jane's contact information. Seconds after she offered it, a text came in. "This is my number. Call any time. I'll answer any questions you have."

"Thank you."

"Will you keep me updated?" Desperation tinged the woman's voice now, causing Jane's suspicions to war with her sympathies. "Please?"

"I will." But only as much as she felt comfortable sharing.

Emma set her pet on the floor and stood. They said their goodbyes, leaving Jane alone with Rolex, who slinked out from under the table to sniff every surface the corgi had dared to touch, often pawing the floor with curiosity. Or disgust. No, definitely curiosity, maybe.

"My first official case," she told him with a grin. Then she texted Fiona about Hagger, and the grandmother responded right away, telling her she'd already fired Hagger and hired new representation. Thank goodness! Now, to call Conrad and tell him the good news or not?

No need to deliberate further. Not. Not yet, anyway. Better to follow her leads first. After a shower and very late morning rounds, she would visit the bank. She'd share what she learned when Conrad stopped by later.

Oh my. Conrad. Stopping by. Later. Jane licked her lips. Perhaps… maybe… possibly…she should whip together a nice dinner for him. Or them. Whatever. Their first date could take place here, where she felt most comfortable. Because, now that she considered it further, dating him maybe wasn't so terrible of an idea. Emma was all kinds of right. No one with a brain would open up to a city boy. For reasons. Good ones! Jane wouldn't, that was for sure. Bottom line? Conrad absolutely, positively was a city boy. Temporary at best.

Think about it. The special agent lived in downtown Atlanta an hour away. And in a fancy condo with no personality that didn't fit him in the slightest no less. As if Jane could *ever* fall in love with such a man. Like him, yes. But not love. Which meant he'd never activate the Ladling curse, turning a talking tree's prediction that she would forever bear the name "Miss Regret Cursed the Fourth" into a reality —long story. Short version: Her heart remained safe.

Conrad wouldn't devastate Rolex by bailing when the little darling needed him most. And no, she wasn't acting like the romance novel heroines she loved to read about, giving herself an excuse to keep seeing the guy who would later turn out to be the love of her life. That was *so* not what was happening here.

Her heart thudded. But, um, was she truly considering taking the next step with Conrad?

Her phone rang, and she leaped on the distraction at warp speed. Spotting the number displayed on the screen, Jane gaped. Someone from the Bank of Aurelian Hills. Seriously? The very place Lucy Chang worked.

Uh, what if Lucy was the one on the other end of the line?

Frowning, Jane tapped the button and pressed the phone to her ear. "Yes, um, hello? This is me. I mean, this is Jane. Jane Ladling. I'm she."

"Hi, Jane. You might not remember me, but I'm Lucy Chang. A loan officer at the Bank of Aurelian Hills."

Okay, what the heck was even going on right now? Jane thought of a person and boom, they reached out? *Henry Cavill, Henry Cavill, Henry Cavill.* "Yes, I remember you. You worked at my event last night."

"Yes, that's me." Lucy gave a nervous laugh. "I would love to meet with you here at the bank. Today. If it's not too much trouble. I'm willing to work around your schedule."

She wanted to shout, "Yes!" but the oddity of the situation left her speechless. A murder investigation had never gone so seamlessly, and she wasn't sure she liked it.

Lucy lowered her volume, whispering, "Please visit me. There's something you need to know about the murder."

CHAPTER FOUR

"Victory doesn't fall on you like ripe cherries from a tree.
You fight to make it happen."
Lucas "Trick" Robichaud

Jane smoothed the lines of her dress. A cascading floral fit-and-flare with interlocking sections of black and teal. When satisfied with that, she adjusted the hat pinned to her crown. The little beauty possessed sprigs of both blue and green flowers to match. All right. Nothing out of place. With a large purse dangling from her shoulder, she soared into the ornate lobby of the premier bank for Aurelian Hills.

A bell tinkled as she went from bright daylight and cold to subdued lighting and warmth. Up ahead, an electronic banner flashed the words *Serving Your Needs Since 1832.* The only nod to the twenty-first century. Other than the state-of-the-art security, of course, hidden throughout for discretion.

No expense had been spared on the marble flooring and pillars, or the golden lions that guarded the vault. Even the bars between tellers and customers were said to be encrusted with flakes of gold. Sadly, such rumors had only led to the real life hotsy-totsy robberies of decades past.

Jane ignored the vibrating cell in a purse pocket and strolled deeper inside the building. No doubt it was Ashley Katz from the Headliner again; over the last hour, the woman had called repeatedly, not taking the hint when Jane failed to answer, too busy for an interview right now.

At a reception desk littered with tiny pumpkins sat an older security guard with the thickest mustache in history. Per Lucy's instructions, Jane stopped there to sign in.

Perhaps a wee bit too loudly, she proclaimed, "I'm here because I have an appointment with Ms. Chang. For a loan. Well, a potential loan." Because she refused to lie, she would, in fact, be filling out the paperwork for said loan. If, by some miracle she got it, she'd either turn it down or use it to purchase cameras for the Valley of Dolls.

The guard frowned at her but also waved to a waiting area with uncomfortable looking chairs. "Have a seat. I'm sure she'll be with you shortly."

Wonderful. Jane would use the time to text Beau and draft questions for Tony's business partner, Devin Hagger. Before driving to the bank, she'd contacted his office to make an appointment. They were scheduled to meet tomorrow morning at 10:00.

Preparation had never been more important.

Jane eased into a seat. Getting as cozy as possible, she withdrew her phone from her clutch. Yep. The earlier call had indeed come from Ashley Katz.

Sighing, she typed the message to Beau: *Where are my crime scene photos, Bo-Bo?????? (Okay, the nickname was supposed to be a punishment for your terrible breech of manners, but it's so cute I think we should run with it.) Also, can you do morning rounds for me tomorrow, since you'll be doing patrol anyway?????*

I'll pay you in the form of a meal and great conversation since you won't accept my money.

Beaudyguard: *Two meals, and Bo-Bo says deal.*

She snorted. Dang, she treasured this amazing man.

Jane: *Done! Now get me those photos.*

Beaudyguard: *You'll have them by tomorrow morning, promise.*

Why the hold up? Was he afraid she'd see something disturbing?

Inquiries for later. Time to craft those hard-hitting questions for Hagger. Except, Lucy exited an office at the end of a narrow hallway. A beauty in her late twenties, with sleek black hair and rich brown eyes. She wore a dark gray pencil skirt and a black-and-white striped top—and no wedding ring.

Hmm. A potential match for one of Beau's friends, perhaps? In Jane's mind, Beau himself was already paired with Eunice Park…who continued to ignore her calls. But that was something else she needed to put on hold for now. If Jane remembered correctly, the slightly older Lucy had been kind to everyone in school, no matter their social status. Or lack thereof, in Jane's case. In other words, perfect companion material.

"Jane Ladling?" The other woman flashed a practiced, almost brittle smile. "Why don't you come on back?" With the precision of a military sergeant, she pivoted on her high heels and returned to the office, her spine ramrod straight.

Confused by the frosty greeting, Jane followed. Had coming here been a mistake? For all she knew, Lucy had hoped to trap her into making some kind of confession about Fiona and Beau.

Jane entered a small space filled with pictures of an adorable chonky, calico cat. Okay. Forget the greeting and the suspicion.

This woman was definitely on the up and up, and a perfect potential match for one of Beau's friends. Anyone who loved their feline to such a degree received a gold star seal of approval.

Wait. Her sudden lack of suspicion for the loan officer made her suspicions resurge with a vengeance.

"Please, shut the door and have a seat." All professional politeness, Lucy sank into a swivel chair in front of a computer and stacked a set of already stacked papers and folders. "We'll get started."

Once the thick wooden door clicked into place, Jane sank into her own chair on the other side of the desk. She withdrew a pen and her trusty notebook *Truth Be Told*, ready to take notes. "Why am I here?"

Just like that, the other woman's air of professionalism evaporated. She deflated, seeming to melt over her keyboard. "Thank you so much for coming. I've been at my wit's end... haven't known what to do or who to trust."

Wow. What a change! "Why don't you start by telling me how you think I can help?"

Lucy wrung her fingers. "Rumor is, you're something of an expert sleuth. So, if anyone can clear my good name, it's you. And I need to clear my good name. I'm afraid the authorities will try to pin Tony's murder on me. That's why I'd like to hire you to prove my innocence."

You've got to be kidding me. "Why do you believe this?"

"Well, you've solved two cases already."

Uh... "I assure you, I'm very aware of my own talents. I meant, why do you think the agents will target you?"

The beauty picked up a pencil and tapped the end against the desk. "Last month, I hired Tony to force my ex-boyfriend to return Cartier—my cat. Oliver stole her from my house, just to hurt me. But Tony only sent the jerk a typo-ridden letter, then tried to charge me two thousand dollars for it."

Oh yes. That sounded very much like a Tony Miller

special. The man had attempted to charge Jane four hundred dollars for a ten second phone call. "Did you pay him anything?"

Her lips pressed together in disgust. "I refused to give him a dime." The disgust morphed into uncertainty. "But maybe I should have done it. All night I read up on the three Cs of motive."

Ugh. C. The worst of letters. Jane had dated three men in her twenty-six years. Clint, Christopher, and now Conrad, who was beyond lucky she hadn't sworn off all C-named people after the first two jerks had shredded her heart. "Please. Do tell."

"Well, they are coin, contempt and carnality," Lucy said, "and I have two out of three. It's only a matter of time before GBH wonders if I hired someone to kill Tony simply to get out of paying my bill."

"You might be right." Jane had to be honest. Even she was speculating about the possibility. *Had* Lucy hired someone to kill Tony to get out of paying her bill. How better to get a little payback in the process? There were definitely elements of coin—the unpaid bill—and contempt for the sleazy lawyer who'd tried to coerce Lucy into giving him money. The banker was right; in the eyes of law enforcement, she lacked only carnality. Talk about a bona fide motive. "Do you have a criminal record?"

"No. I absolutely do not. But… I kind of, possibly, might have, maybe committed a teensy, tiny, hardly worth mentioning felony recently." The other woman chewed on her bottom lip. "I broke into Oliver's house and stole my cat back, okay? But that was a crusade for justice!"

"Agreed. A true act of heroism."

Brightening at the show of support, Lucy shifted in her seat. "Right?" Within seconds, however, she sagged into herself. "There's more to my story. See, Tony attempted to blackmail me at your party. He said I needed to give him information about his ex-wife or he would provide Oliver with proof of what I'd done."

Jane scribbled her thoughts as swiftly as possible, doing her best to hide her astonishment. Aurelian Hills truly was a hotbed of illegal activity. "What kind of information did Tony seek?"

"Well, he wanted to know how much money Ms. Miller had in her account. How often she made withdrawals. If she'd used her bank card at any restaurants in the city."

All good questions. Jane wouldn't mind knowing those answers either. Had Tony's obsession with finding out if Emma had a boyfriend driven his actions all evening?

"What did you tell him?" she asked.

Affront tightened the loan officer's expression. "Nothing," she said as her spine went ramrod straight. "First, I don't even know that kind of information off the top of my head. Second, that's a violation of at least three banking secrecy laws and privacy statutes."

Or Lucy had told him everything and now covered her tracks. "How did Tony react to your refusal?"

"He was furious." Her chin quivered. "Then he caught sight of someone, cursed, and gave chase."

Yes, that tracked with what Jane herself had seen. "Any idea why he'd want to follow this mystery person?"

"None. I didn't recognize him." Her eyes went soft and dreamy. "Trust me, I would have remembered meeting him."

Oh? "Describe him, please."

"Certainly." Lucy propped her elbows on the desktop. "He was over six feet, black, with short, curly hair and the richest brown eyes. Obviously he likes to work out. He wore a suit that fit him perfectly, a fedora hat, white tie and spats. There was a slight air of gentlemanly danger around him. Honestly, he was the kind of guy who makes you wish he'd pick you up and carry you away."

"Yes, I'm familiar with the type." And good to know Lucy liked muscular men, because Trick, Isaac and Holden packed major heat. But. Jane didn't recall seeing such a buffet of masculinity at the event—or in the tent after the murder occurred—and she employed expert level observation skills sometimes.

Had Fedora purposely avoided the authorities? Had he participated in the game or come for a genuine murder? Surely other people had spotted him. Had he purchased a ticket or snuck in? She would ask Trick, her ticket taker.

Perhaps someone had even snapped photos of Fedora. Either way, Jane figured she'd catch sight of him when she watched the security feed. Later. After she visited the Gilded Scissor Beauty Shop across the street. At the party, the bank and the salon had been neighbors. Maybe the stylists remembered the guy.

"Do you know of anyone else who might have wanted to hurt Tony?" Jane asked.

Lucy nodded with enthusiasm. "I've given this tons of thought. I think Devin Hagger, Tony's partner, might be involved. He visited my booth and demanded to know what Tony said to me."

Hmm. Both Emma and Lucy had happily tossed Hagger under the bus, which made him seem less guilty and them more so. Could the two women be working together? "I'll be speaking with Mr. Hagger tomorrow, don't worry. If you'll send me a copy of every photo you took at the event, as well as your correspondence with Tony, I'll be better equipped to deal with the partner."

"Yes, yes. Will do. So you'll do it? You'll take my case?" Lucy anchored her elbows on the desk and leaned forward.

"You'll find the real killer and prove my innocence? I can pay you. Not much, but something."

Jane had wondered if Emma sought to inject herself into the investigation to manipulate any evidence. Now, she had to wonder the same thing about Lucy. But. Same deal. Since Jane planned to look into things, anyway, why not take advantage of this all-access pass to a suspect?

"Yes, I'll take the case," she announced. "I want the truth, and that's what I'll deliver. All I request in return is a promise for playdates with Cartier once the culprit is caught." As long as Lucy turned out to be innocent, of course. "I have a cat, too. His name is Rolex, and he's the sweetest, most precious darling in the world." Considering the endearing way he'd reacted to Cheddar, he obviously desired a friend. His wish, her command.

A smile bloomed over the loan officer's lovely face. "I knew you were the right person for this job. And Rolex sounds amazing. I'm in love with him already."

"He *is* amazing." She handed over her phone to show off a few dozen photos. "If you scroll to the left quickly, it'll seem like you're watching him live and in person eating a bug and being adorable."

Lucy oohed and awed with the appropriate amount of awe, both delighting Jane and fueling her suspicions. Another suspect's possible attempt to butter her up?

When a text chimed from the device, the other woman's cheeks reddened, and she returned the phone in a hurry. "Um. I didn't mean to read it, I promise."

Uh-oh. Jane's stomach churned as she checked the screen, unsure what to expect.

Agent Spice: *By the way, I'm taking your silence on the subject as a yes, I should come over tonight and plan to stay a while. I promise not to kiss you unless you ask nicely—or demand it.*

Oh, sweet goodness. The man certainly knew how to

steal the air from her lungs. "Yes. Well." She cleared her throat, opting to respond to Conrad once her brain came back online. "He's kind of my, um, boyfriend." The once forbidden word was getting easier to say. "We're dating. Well, not *dating* dating. Not yet. Maybe not ever. I'm still deciding. But I'm leaning toward saying yes. We're together and we're exclusive." *Shut up. You're babbling.*

"I understand," Lucy assured her with a firm nod. For some reason, the assurance struck Jane as genuine. "I once dated-not-dated a guy I only ever spoke with through text. Our relationship lasted three months."

Could there be a more perfect opening for matchmaking? "So you're single right now?"

"I am. After Oliver, I may never date again."

Ha! Jane used to say the same thing. Then she met Conrad. An honorable guy had the power to change everything. Well, not everything. He would never convince her to consider the ultimate prize: a future together. She couldn't let him. Nope. Whatever happened, her course was set. City boys and cursed cemetery girls didn't get forever, remember?

Again, she cleared her throat. "If you'll give me a loan application, I'll get going. Just so you know, I don't actually want the loan, I don't think, so maybe don't approve it. But either way, this will help us maintain our cover."

"Yes, yes. Smart thinking. Honesty is always the best policy."

"Agreed." She meant that. Did the other woman?

Lucy gathered the necessary pages, stuffed them inside a folder, wrote something on a Post It she adhered to the top, then handed everything over. "Please call me anytime. That's my private number."

She stacked the folder against *Truth Be Told,* crammed both in her oversized purse, and stood. "Let me know if you recall anything else about Tony."

"Will do. And Jane? Thank you."

"What can I say? I'm a sucker for justice." She let herself out of the office and strode from the building, entering the warm, sunlit afternoon. Cars zipped across Prospect Street.

As she strolled along the sidewalk, heading for the Gilded Scissor Beauty Shop, her phone vibrated. She paused in the shadows under an awning, out of the way of any passersby, and freed the device. Ugh. The Headliner again.

"Ignore," she muttered, kicking into motion. In less than a minute, she was striding inside the salon. Unfortunately, neither the owner nor the guy who'd helped operate the booth had arrived for the day.

Far from done with her quest for info, Jane headed to the Treasure Room. A showplace for local crafters that had quickly grown into a tea shop, book nook and event center. The owner's booth had possessed a bird's eye view of Lucy's. Along the way, Jane passed the Cave of Wonders Hobby Shop, aka the Treasure's Room's fiercest rival.

"Hello," she called, waving to the two patrons outside.

The pair ignored her. Oh well. Outside of events at the cemetery, most townsfolk brushed her off. She'd always been a bit of an oddball, she supposed.

Next door, ill-played piano tinkled out of the Grand Dame Dance Academy as Mrs. Dehew banged on ancient keys. At some point, every child of Aurelian Hills had either shuffled along the dance floor or practiced scales in that building.

Jane's phone rang as she turned a corner. She swallowed a groan, halfway expecting Ashley Katz again. Or even Hannah Thorton, the Treasure Room's owner, hoping to set up a meeting and hire her to solve the mystery of Tony's death. For all Jane knew, *every* party attendee worked together to slay the attorney and now each one awaited a chance to cast blame on Hagger. Which wasn't exactly a nonstarter.

Stranger things had happened. Namely, three murders in a handful of months, each taking place within the same cemetery.

Braced for a shock, Jane freed the phone yet again. Oh! Dread morphed into relief and happiness when she caught sight of Fiona's name.

"Hey you," she said, pressing the cell to her ear. "I'm so glad you called. I have so much to tell you."

"Jane! Jane!" her friend screeched, all kinds of panic in the undertone.

Oh, no, no, no. What had occurred? Her heart thundered in her chest. "Fiona, what's wrong?"

"Jane, stop whatever you're doing and come to the hospital. Nothing has ever been more important in your entire life."

The blood rushed from her head, igniting a high-pitched roar in her ears. "Who's hurt?" Fiona herself? Had Conrad been shot on the job? Had Beau gotten into some kind of altercation with an intruder at the cemetery? What, what?

"It's Raymond." Fiona whimpered. "He's had a heart attack."

CHAPTER FIVE

"Don't just play the game. Play to win."
Isaac Redding, security expert

Jane squeezed Fiona's trembling hand. They occupied a small room in Pinetum Regional, the rural hospital shared by two neighboring communities, where Sheriff Moore slept on a bed. He wore a paper-thin gown and had wires and tubes extending from a plethora of locations. Usually tanned skin was pallid, a blue tracery of veins visible.

Beau and Conrad had arrived minutes after Jane. The two sat in cushioned chairs by the only window, marveling in hushed tones about small towns and the number of visitors allowed to congregate in each private space. In the background, a steady *beep-beep* played on repeat.

Fiona offered a return squeeze. "Raymond's going to be okay. He is," she said, but she didn't sound convinced. "The pain medication has made him extra tired, that's all."

"What happened?" Jane asked, doing her best to mask her growing tremors.

"Well, after I left your house, I paid him a visit at his request." Her friend licked her lips. "He had missed dinner, you see, so I went straight to his kitchen to prepare my famous blueberry pancakes."

Lucky man. There was no meal more perfect than those pancakes. Jane's most favorite food in all the world. A treasure worth more than gold.

"We ate and giggled like silly teenagers and—" Fiona's lower lip trembled. Tears filled her dark eyes. "The next thing I knew, he was on the floor, clutching his chest, trying his darnedest to die on me. I've never been so frightened in my life. I called 911, and here we are."

"Oh, Fee. I'm so sorry."

Fiona rasped, "My incredible food caused too much excitement. I think I'm done with baking for good."

What! No! "Don't say that. Don't ever say that again." Such a horrendous idea should *never* be entertained. "If anything, those pancakes gave him something to live for."

"Maybe." Fiona sniffled. "But probably not." Her voice dropped to a low whisper. "What if he doesn't recover? What if... Jane, what if I killed him? What if you aren't the only one who's cursed?"

A barbed lump grew in her throat, restricting her airway. Did Fiona love the sheriff? The grandmother had certainly crushed on him for years. Ever since his wife had left him for another man and another town. And what if the Ladling curse *had* transferred to her dearest friend through their prolonged association?

If the kind woman who'd comforted Jane after every heartbreak now suffered because of their association...

Her airways constricted a bit more. Though the curse itself focused on romantic love, stating every Ladling female was destined to lose her chosen partner—whether it took a day or a decade—Jane had lost so much more. Her mother, who often forgot her very existence. Same with her father. Both Grandma Lily and Pops had died far too early.

Only a handful of blood relatives remained. A smattering of half brothers and half sisters who weren't part of her life. None wanted to be. Jane had the people in this room, plus Rolex, Trick, Isaac and Holden, and no others. The eight she'd chosen to welcome into her orbit. If Sheriff Moore died, Fiona might waste away of a shattered heart, leaving Jane with only six friends and an endless supply of guilt.

Who would the curse cull next?

Wait. How had it gotten so hot, so fast in the room? When had her throat finished closing, making it *impossible* to breathe? For that matter, why was her heart punching her ribs? And how was her blood ice cold, despite that awful heat?

"Jane?" Fiona cried. "Jane, what's wrong? You're turning purple. Doctor! Doctor! Help!"

Conrad and Beau leaped from their chairs. The special agent rushed over to Jane, muttering to the others, "She'll be fine, I've got this," while Beau went straight to Fiona.

Jane's boyfriend performed his patented move, slinging an arm around her waist. He led her into the hallway and pressed her back against a wall.

"Inhale, sweetheart." Ever gentle, he gathered her hair with one hand, holding the bundle over her shoulder, and stroked his knuckles up and down her sternum with the other. "Exhale. Inhale."

"You think I'm not trying?" she croak-yelled, glaring anywhere but Conrad, searching for an avenue of escape. She needed to leave this hospital now, now, now. She needed...she...

"Look at me." He repositioned, cupping her jawline, saying, "Look at me, Jane."

Oh, that coaxing tone! Did he have any idea how irritating it was? But okay, fine, she obeyed, meeting his eyes for a split second, because manners. Then she did it again, only longer. And again. Suddenly, she couldn't peer elsewhere. He beamed all kinds of kindness and understanding at her, igniting tendrils of calm. Those tendrils coiled around her panic and choked the life from it.

She sucked in oxygen. "I hate that this is happening. The curse is up to its old tricks, only it's branching out, determined to claim new victims. Poor Sheriff Moore. Just when things started to blossom with Fee, snap! Not so fast, it says. You might want to back out of our arrangement now, Conrad, before it's too late. No telling what the curse will do to you."

He traced his thumbs over the rise of her cheeks. "All you see is never all there is, sweetheart."

"You're giving me a riddle?" Was he for real right now? "Do you not care that a good man might die for a bad reason? Especially when the town really, really needs him. As you probably noticed, crime rates have recently spiked."

"Yes," he replied, his tone wry. "The *town* needs him."

She drummed her fists against his chest. "Stop making light of a serious situation." Wow. His muscles. Drumming turned into petting. Those peaks and valleys felt like granite. They spoke of strength. Strength brought more comfort.

"Trust me. I'm being *very* serious." He bent his head to brush the tip of his nose against hers. "Did you wear your listening ears today, Jane Ladling?"

"Probably not," she told him, forlorn.

"Too bad. You're going to hear what I'm saying, anyway." The most divine heat radiated from his hands. "The sheriff is already recovering. With some time and effort, he'll be fully restored. You did not cause this. Fiona did not cause this. Neither one of you is cursed."

But... "You can't know that."

"What I know is this. The Ladling curse *is* real. Because you believe it." Gentle tone, harsh words. He kissed her brow. "But I'm determined. I'll prove the curse has no power over you."

No. No! He was wrong. Or possibly right? Maybe? She did believe the very wise words Grandma Lily once told her, when she'd come home from school crying because no one wanted to be her friend. *Jay Bird, you can't make people like you. But you can be the best possible you. One day, your kindness and generosity will come back to you. Everything always comes back.*

But, but…this wasn't the same. It couldn't be. Could it? No, no. It couldn't. Next Conrad would repeat what Fiona often told her. That fear fueled the Ladling curse, making it a self-fulfilling prophecy.

Jane opened her mouth to protest, but no sound emerged. Argh! So part of her remained unconvinced in his wrongness, okay? But the other part of her was much smarter. Loss equaled pain. Intelligent people avoided pain.

He must have detected the resistance in her expression because he heaved a heavy sigh and pressed his forehead against hers. "Everything will be all right, sweetheart. I'm determined. The curse is our dragon. We'll slay it and create our own personal fairy tale."

That. That did it. She had already picked out a name for their fairy tale and everything. The Cemetery Maiden and the Prince of Spices.

Relief showered her, and she melted against him. "Our tale will inspire the masses for eons to come."

"Probably longer." He placed a light kiss on her lips. "Dragon slaying is my specialty. You might not know this, but I'm a pretty scary guy. I've already frightened the sheriff into recovering faster."

Jane gave a little snort. Realizing she'd found humor in a non-humorous situation, she pursed her lips.

"It's okay to smile and laugh, even at times like this. Especially at times like this." Conrad continued on before she could respond. "I spoke with the doc before I came to the room, and he assured me Raymond is walking out of here. He'll need to make some lifestyle changes, but he's a resolute man. With Fiona by his side, he'll be more dogged than ever."

"You're right." *Of course* everything would turn out well for Fiona and the sheriff. They were too wonderful not to get their happily ever after.

Someone cleared her throat, alerting Jane to another presence.

Conrad eased his face from hers, but retained his hold on her. "Yes?" he asked the intruder.

"I'm here to check your grandfather's vitals," the woman said to Jane.

Ah. A nurse. Her ID badge read Mindy. The fifty-something heroine of medicine wore pink scrubs and a kind smile as she motioned to the door Jane and Conrad now blocked. Oops. But, uh, grandfather?

The special agent didn't correct the assumption, so neither did she. What a perfect opportunity to further the case! Did Emma have access to these facilities? For that matter, had any opioids been reported stolen lately?

"I'm a granddaughter, yes," Jane stated. Not a lie. Both of her parents possessed a father, and those fathers, though deceased, were her grandfathers. "I'd like to know what medications you're giving our patient." The questioning had to kick off somewhere. "Any opioids?"

Mindy blinked. "I'll have to check his chart. My shift just started, so this is my first examination of him. But, if I had to guess, I'd say no. For a myocardial infarction, we usually start with aspirin and nitroglycerin. Is there a reason you ask? Is he allergic?"

Conrad lightly pinched Jane's chin before releasing her, letting her know her sleuthing hadn't gone unnoticed. "No allergy to our knowledge," he told the nurse, straightening and opening the sheriff's door. "You deal with the sleeping patient. I'll handle the curious granddaughter."

Without another word, Mindy soared past them and entered the room. Fiona and Beau exited soon after, the sheriff's grumbles following them. "Enough with the poking and prodding already."

At the sound of his gruff voice, Jane grinned. Yeah, he was gonna be all right.

Their group relocated to a waiting room, where chairs were scattered about. Two other guests sat before a TV mounted on the wall, watching what looked to be a home renovation show. In the opposite corner, next to a drink station and vending machines, was a round table topped by a half-finished puzzle. A chest of plastic toys rested against one of the legs.

Beau helped Fiona into a seat and eased beside her, patting her hand. Jane took the spot on her other side, with Conrad plopping next to Jane.

"Tell me why you want to know about the sheriff's medications," the agent commanded for her ears alone.

And betray client confidentiality? "No, thank you."

"Very well. I'll guess. You've spoken to Miller's ex-wife."

Dang it! Nothing got by this man. Rather than confirm or deny it, she said, "Do you know if any opioids have been reported stolen from this hospital? Or Aurelian Hills Medical Clinic, for that matter." Emma's place of employment.

He peered up at the ceiling, as if praying for divine guidance. "I shouldn't tell you. But I will because the information can be gleaned outside of GBH thanks to the Headliner. And because I won't be able to come by the cottage tonight as planned. I have to return to the office. This can serve as my apology."

"In that case, apology accepted." When had he decided to stop dissuading her from investigating and start encouraging her? Because she liked this development. "*If* the information is juicy enough, of course."

"Of course. Brat," he huffed with affection. "The clinic doesn't keep any opioids on hand. However, Pinetum Regional does. Last week a vial was, in fact, reported stolen. The same drug found in Miller's system. And before you ask, Nurse Miller doesn't have clearance here. Dr. Garcia and Dr. Price do. They attended your party, as well, so they are being interviewed today."

Dr. Garcia worked at the clinic with Emma. He could've swiped the medication for his employee. But... "Dr. Price?" Never heard of him.

"What's this? Do I know something about Aurelian Hills that you don't?" A twinkle entered Conrad's whiskey eyes. "Dr. Price moved to town about six months ago. He works in a rival clinic. Med and Care."

Well, well. The last two murders had been committed by newcomers. Would the pattern continue? "Describe him, please," she invited.

He moaned but said, "Six foot four. Black, with a muscular build. Short hair. Brown eyes. No tattoos or noticeable scars."

Hmm. Sounded like the dreamboat Lucy had spotted. "This is a serious investigation, Conrad. Details matter. When you say short hair, are we talking a standard buzz cut? Or something with a fade? Any curls?" Lucy mentioned curls. "And by brown, do you mean a deep sable, classic honey, or rich chestnut?"

His mouth opened and closed. "Yes?"

Men! The world's worst observers. "I don't recall seeing the name Price on the guest list."

"Lucas Robichaud added his name to your roster the night of the party. Says the guy bought a ticket at the door."

Um, who? "Lucas Robichaud?"

"I think you call him Trick."

Oh. So that was his name. Wait. A last-minute decision to attend a fancy, costumed event? Suspicious! Jane added Dr. Price to her list of suspects, as well as Dr. Garcia, then double checked the others. Emma, Lucy, and Devin Hagger. Yep. All belonged. No changes necessary.

With such a minefield of probable guiltiness, something good had to blow up soon.

She really, really needed to watch her own security footage ASAP. And touch base with the booth operators. And also check out the Headliner online and finally speak with the reporter.

Hey! Speaking of, Jane spotted a copy of the new Headliner Weekly on the table beside Conrad. Leaning over, she swiped up the printed page to check it out. Anything about the murder?

The headline read "Cemetery Owner Dead Quiet." The article—written by Ms. Ashley Katz—went on to discuss the author's determination to unmask Tony's killer.

Great! An amateur was horning in on Jane's territory. What started in a cemetery, should stay in a cemetery. At least Ms. Katz hadn't mentioned Fiona or Beau as suspects.

On that note, Jane tossed the paper aside, whispering to Conrad, "Are you-know-who still suspects?" She didn't want anyone to overhear this part of the conversation. Give her friend another worry? No thanks.

Conrad leveled a what-do-you-think look on her. Enough said. Or not said. Yep, Fiona and Beau were still suspects.

"Jane Eleanor Ladling," Fiona announced, banging the arm of her chair. Had she overheard the conversation, after all? "You've got to leave. Go on now. Get."

What! Abandon her favorite person in the world? The kind woman who'd held her hand at every funeral, even those she'd hosted for her deceased dolls? The cherished friend who'd dried her tears and kissed her booboos? Never! "Hardly. I'm staying with you."

The older woman gave a clipped shake of her head. "You are leaving, and that's that. I'm already decided. You are solving this murder. With you leading the charge, victory is assured. Raymond can stop stressing and recover much faster."

Conrad cleared his throat and spread his arms wide, all *do you see the special agent sitting right here?*

Fiona waved a dismissive hand in his direction, as if he were making a joke. "Don't worry," she told Jane. "The boys are here, and they are happy to take care of me."

Conrad grumbled under his breath, and Beau folded his lips behind his teeth, clearly trying not to laugh.

"Aren't you, boys?" Fee demanded.

"Yes, ma'am," the two piped up in unison.

A sense of purpose and unshakable determination washed over Jane. Fiona was right. She *must* do this. For her friends, and the sheriff. For Team Truth. For the Garden. For the entire town!

Jane kissed the other woman's cheek. "Rest assured, I will cross any line to accomplish our goal. Nothing and no one is safe."

"I'll pretend I didn't hear that," Conrad said.

Reaching out, she patted Beau's hand. "Keep me updated. And don't forget to send me those crime scene photos as promised."

"I won't." A firm nod accompanied his words.

Conrad piped up again, saying, "And I won't try to stop you. It's never done me any good. You're welcome, by the way."

Twisting, she focused on her boyfriend. He appeared resigned. Her heart began to pound, and she wasn't sure why. No, not true. She knew why. She was putting on her big girl panties and canceling their date. This wasn't the time for romance.

As if he sensed her intention, he slid a strong, calloused hand to her nape and wound strands of her hair around his fingers. To keep her in place? Warmth cascaded down her spine, and her lips parted.

His pupils expanded, spilling over those whiskey-rich irises. "I won't let you do it," he rasped with a rough voice. "You aren't backing out of our date. If the sheriff's condition has taught me anything, it's to seize the moment while I can." He tightened his hold. "I'll pick you up tomorrow at seven. Say yes."

Tremors invaded her limbs. A dinner. In public. While dressed up. Engaging in flirty conversation. All kinds of romantic. More than being frivolous at a serious time, she risked falling deeper into like with him.

She risked everything.

City boy, city boy, city boy.

Curse, curse, curse.

The Cemetery Maiden and the Prince of Spices.

In the end, she croaked, "Yes."

CHAPTER SIX

"If kale can be a super food, victory is always achievable."
Raymond Moore, Sheriff of Aurelian Hills

Jane changed into her most comfortable pajamas and padded to the living room, where she settled on the couch and draped her lower half with Grandma Lily's knitted throw. A glass of sweet tea waited on the coffee table.

Determined, she opened her laptop. She'd promised to work this case like a boss, and she would. Waste time stewing about the sheriff? No. Worry wouldn't help him or the investigation. Nor would she consider the gleam of satisfaction in Conrad's eyes after she'd agreed to go on a first date with him. If she did, she'd start shivering again. Instead, she planned to study the most minute details of the cemetery's security footage.

"You ready for this?" she asked Rolex as he cuddled up beside her.

He yawned and stretched, flaring the cutest little murder mittens in all the world. She'd take that as a yes.

Very well. "We begin."

For what seemed both an endless and too quick an eternity, Jane watched two hours of video. As planned, she examined every detail. Took notes. Restarted. Rewound. Rewatched. Fast forwarded. What she learned? Aurelian Hill was more of a hotbed of scandal than she'd realized.

Leo Ewers had kissed the second Mrs. Ewers while the third Mrs. Ewers searched for a game clue at a booth. Resident hoarder Wren Coburn apparently liked to collect items belonging to other residents. Taylor Milton committed the worst offense of all, throwing his trash on the ground, dirtying the immaculate Garden. First a gum wrapper, then a candy bar wrapper, then a soda can.

Finally, Jane spotted the beefcake Lucy and Conrad had mentioned. Six feet four of muscles, exactly as advertised, in a stylish 1920s suit. A quick search of the Med and Care Clinic's website showcased a picture of a smiling Dr. Frederick Price, confirming the beefcake's identity.

After spending good money to purchase a ticket at the door, the doctor had slinked from shadow to shadow, enjoying nothing. *Very unusual behavior, Dr. Price.* Of course, his name shot to the top spot on her suspect list.

Why not stop by his clinic after her visit with Mr. Hagger tomorrow and ask a few questions?

Jane scribbled a reminder in her notebook, then turned her attention to Lucy to track the loan officer's every move. Hmm. She'd left the bank's booth five minutes and thirteen seconds before the scream rang out. Enough time to rush to the Valley of Dolls and commit a murder?

Emma, who'd worn a dark purple flapper dress and black boa, spoke with Lucy about ten minutes before the loan officer's mysterious departure. Had Emma searched for a game clue—or had the two women plotted to take out a mutual enemy?

When a group of three clue hunters converged on the stall next to Lucy's, Dr. Garcia among them, Emma moved on to the booth staffed by Daisy's, a diner famous for magical chicken noodle soup and the universe's most delicious hand cut chips. No other sign of Emma or Lucy until after the murder occurred. Neither acted guilty or fearful, only confused.

If Jane remembered correctly, Dr. Garcia had appeared pale and shaky after the discovery of the body. She scrolled through the photos she'd snapped inside the tent. Yep. There. She'd captured a moment the doctor looked ready to vomit.

What are you hiding? Had he aided Emma, as suspected? Perhaps he'd resented Tony for a personal reason. If Tony had threatened some sort of medical malpractice suit, the doctor could have taken him out before any evidence came to light.

What Jane knew beyond a doubt: Tony's killer hadn't picked the Valley of the Dolls by accident. Anyone who'd paid attention to the last investigation knew she had no cameras out there. Someone with a fake name—the murderer, no doubt—had posted about it on the Headliner, no doubt thinking to widen the pool of suspects.

On the screen, Jane caught sight of Devin Hagger. Short and round, with a comb-over. While he'd looked dangerous in person, he lacked charisma on film. In the first frame, a revolving camera captured the tail end of his conversation with Tony. Hagger seemed to snap a retort or insult before storming away. Exactly as Beau had described. Though there was no sign of Beau nearby to clue her in about his mysterious activities. Or even Emma, who'd also witnessed this event.

Tony headed in the opposite direction of Hagger, soon getting lost in the darkness.

In the second frame, less than a minute before Fiona's

scream, Hagger leaned against a great magnolia tree, smoking a cigarette next to a sign that read No Smoking On Premises. Well. Clearly he believed rules did not apply to him.

He climbed her list too, joining Dr. Price in the number one spot.

Hagger could have murdered Tony, sprinted to the tree, and lit up to create an illusion of relaxation, as well as an alibi. His motive seemed pretty clear—getting rid of a problematic co-worker. It was a well-known fact Tony had lost a ton of cases lately. No doubt Hagger had been eager to end their association to preserve his reputation and business.

Oh! Who was *this*? Jane rewound the footage and paused on the image of a lean, mean guy with longish brown hair and a goatee. She didn't recall seeing him in the welcome tent, either before or after the murder. Had he snuck in and out? Committed the crime and bailed, perhaps?

After printing his picture, she replayed the video from the start, searching only for him.

Well, well, well. Definitely a sneaker-inner. Goatee showed up in many of the same frames as Emma, but always lurking in the shadows somewhere behind her, looking as mad as a hornet. Learning his identity became priority one.

A yawn overtook Jane, nearly cracking her jaw. Goodness gracious. Look at the time. Four in the morning. She'd missed dinner and a midnight snack. At least Rolex had a new feeder timed to provide his meals.

She checked her text messages. Yikes! So many!

Fionality: *Raymond is demanding to go home. Obviously, he's his usual self again. Cardiologist wants to monitor him for another couple days and run some tests. Okay if we skip knitting this week? I plan to stay at his house and pamper him back to health.*

Jane replied with gushing assurance and a thousand exclamation points.

Agent Spice: *Don't even think about canceling our date, sweetheart. I have something very special planned...*

She gulped and read on.

Beaudyguard: *I'm in the middle of something, so Trick is coming by in the morning to patrol the grounds. Also, rumor has it the Waynes have returned from "vacation" with Hotchkins.*

Ugh. The widow Tiffany Hotchkins and siblings Robby Waynes and Abigail Waynes-Kirkland. A threesome Jane had accused of murder. But then, who *hadn't* she accused? Tiffany wasn't terrible, but the Waynes sucked hardcore. They believed Jane was hiding massive amounts of gold in coffins, thanks to an ancient, gold-worshiping cult known as the Order of Seven and a founding member who graced Jane's family tree. They were the three who'd attempted to dig up a grave.

But dang it, what task occupied Beau's time and attention?

Nurse Emma: *I don't mean to pester you, but I'm scared, Jane. Any updates on my case?*

Unknown Number: *THIS IS ASHLEY KATZ FROM THE HEADLINER. I'M TRYING TO TOUCH BASE WITH YOU TO DISCUSS ANTHONY MILLER'S MURDER. PLEASE CALL ME BACK.*

All caps? Really? Suddenly Jane had zero desire to respond to the woman now or ever. A hack who apparently used salacious headlines to gain readers.

Cartier's Mom: *Hi Jane. It's Lucy. Just letting you know I emailed my interactions with Tony to the address on the Garden's website. I hope that's okay? The file was too big to text. Also, look how cute!!!!! Cartier is wearing the dress I bought her.*

The attached photo revealed the chonky calico in a pink tutu. In Jane's humble opinion, it was a glorious image. And if she didn't buy a tux for Rolex by end of day tomorrow, she needed to rethink her life choices.

Agent Spice: *By the way. I spoke with Hightower about Dr. Price and Dr. Garcia.*

Not reply? Impossible. **Jane:** *And?????????????*

Her phone rang a second later, and she gasped with surprise. *Should have known he'd call.*

Heart thudding, she pressed the cell to her ear. "Hello, Conrad."

"Go to bed, sweetheart. There's still time to grab a few hours of rest." His rumbly voice sent shivers down her spine. "You can investigate tomorrow. Trust me when I say you want to be fully cognizant for our date."

Flutters floated from her belly to her throat. "What are *you* doing awake? And you didn't answer my question."

He ignored the question again. "I'm not sharing anything I've learned until we're seated by the glow of candlelight, eating a meal that isn't nearly as good as yours, and you're batting those baby blues, making me forget my good sense. And even then I'm only sharing the barest tidbits."

"You're blackmailing me?" She smiled slow but sure. "Why, Officer Detective Special Agent Ryan, that's a bona fide crime."

"It is. If you'd like to place me under house arrest, I'll bring my cuffs."

A laugh bubbled up, and she barely managed to tamp it down. "Conrad," she said, meaning to sound stern. Instead, she rasped.

So did he. "Yes, Jane?"

"I…" She licked dry lips. "Thank you. For everything you did today."

"My pleasure." He paused before asking, "Did you find anything while secretly investigating?"

"Maybe. I'll share when I'm ready."

"Fair enough. Now get some sleep. That's an order."

"Sir, yes, sir."

"I like the sound of that."

She chuckled again. They hung up, and she sighed, missing him already. That wasn't

good. Not good at all.

Despite boulder-heavy eyelids, she set the laptop on the coffee table and repositioned on the floor, sitting cross-legged as she opened the file Lucy had sent. Reading the conversations between Tony and his client should provide the perfect distraction. After that, she would draft her questions for Hagger. Then and only then would she grab a few minutes of shuteye before beginning her day. Except, the words soon blurred together and darkness came...

FOR THE SECOND day in a row, a harried knock woke Jane. She jolted upright and blinked rapidly. What–why–*what?*

She sat cross-legged at her coffee table. Plucking a pen from her cheek, she checked the time on her phone. 6:00 a.m. Dang! She should have been up an hour ago, preparing for rounds.

Another series of knocking started up. Bones creaked and muscles protested as she stood. Rubbing her lower back, she shuffled to the front door.

Oh, wow. Morning sunlight proved bright as she peered through the peephole. Trick. But why—never mind. Beau's text. Right. Jane wasn't doing rounds today. Trick had taken over for Beau, who wasn't finished being mysterious.

She opened up, hinges creaking, and welcomed the imposing man inside her living room. He was burly and broad-shouldered, with wavy brown hair, a stubborn chin and the kindest, most adorably ruthless brown eyes.

As soon as he entered, Rolex shot around the corner,

leaped, and scratched Trick's arm, leaving two deep punctures and accompanying claw marks before he darted away. His signature move.

Trick didn't seem the least bit bothered when blood welled. "Beau told me to hand these over first thing." He thrust a thick white envelope her way. "He said he'd save you the time of having to print them yourself."

Curious, she tore open the outer paper and discovered photos of Tony's body. A little squeal of excitement left her, and she rose on her tiptoes to pat Trick's stubbled cheek. "Thank you, thank you!"

For the barest moment, her guest eyed her as if she were a bug under a microscope. "I think you're the only woman alive who thrills over images of a corpse."

Well, it sounded like he didn't know the right women. Hmm. Perhaps she should set him up on a date. He and, say, Lucy could triple with her and Conrad, Beau and Eunice Parks. Depending on the outcome of the investigation, of course.

"Are you single, Trick? Lucas? Trick?" she asked. "Also, I'd love to hear your idea of the perfect mate."

He blinked at her, his mouth opening and closing. A common occurrence in her presence nowadays. His eyes narrowed. "First, I prefer Trick. Second, Beau warned me this might happen."

"I'll take that as a no, and you're open to anyone of my choosing." Excellent. Think of it! An investigator *and* a matchmaker. Jane might be the first of her kind. "Oh! Before I forget. You were the one who checked tickets and IDs at the door. Do you recognize this man?"

She scrambled around until she found the photo of Goatee, then held it up like a prize.

"Oh yeah," Trick said. "He had a ticket with the name

Chris P. Bacon. After refusing to show me his ID, he bounced. He must have snuck back in."

Interesting. Jane had seen the awful name on the list and assumed Mr. Bacon had the worst parents in the world. The fact that he'd refused to hand over his ID... Had he purchased the ticket under a fake name because he'd planned to murder another guest all along? When Plan A failed, he'd resorted to Plan B, sneaking in?

"You wait here while I make us some coffee," she said. "If you share what secret activities Beau has been up to lately, I'll whip you up a nice breakfast, too. All the fixings. Homemade biscuits and sausage gravy. Chicken fried steak with a fried egg topper. Buttermilk pancakes with a frosted butter glaze."

He groaned. "I want to tell you. You have no idea how badly I want to tell you, but he's my friend and I won't betray his confidence. Surely my loyalty earns a biscuit with gravy? Or a casserole for lunch later?"

"You are too cute," she told him with a sincere smile. "You are absolutely going to make someone very happy one day—something I'm willing to help you with as soon as my schedule opens up. But no answers, no casserole. I don't make the rules, I just abide by them. Now go ahead and get comfortable."

The handsome Trick wilted, appearing shredded into a million pieces.

Merciless, Jane hurried off and started the coffee pot. Once she'd passed the security expert a brimming thermos, she saw him out. She only laughed a little when he cast a longing glance toward the kitchen.

After grabbing the photos and her phone, she headed to her room, where Rolex waited. He lounged on the bed, licking one of his paws. Probably delighting in the taste of his enemy.

Jane spent the next five minutes petting him for his adorableness and also texting.

Beau received a nice thank you for the photos and a thumbs down for his secretiveness. She ignored the reporter and her all caps message. She told both of her clients she had several promising leads, then requested the two send her an exact accounting of their activities during the party—a test of sorts. Would they tell the truth or lie? While watching the security footage, she'd taken detailed notes; as soon as their explanations came in, she could do a timestamped comparison.

Conrad…she didn't text again. He would only charm her, and she was now pressed for time. Kind of. Maybe? In only four scant hours—hardly any time at all in the scheme of things—she was supposed to meet with Hagger. And she definitely needed to whip up a batch of cupcakes for the receptionist, Mrs. Butterfield.

Once Jane finished with the attorney, she could visit Dr. Price. According to his website, walk-ins were welcome. Or maybe she'd see Dr. Garcia. Or both! Then, she would finally, at long last, go on that date with her special agent.

She gulped. Well. Guess Conrad didn't need to text to charm and distract her, after all.

CHAPTER SEVEN

"If you're afraid of failure, you've already failed."
Devin Hagger Esquire, attorney at law

Wearing a professional split-neck dress of multi-hued sapphire paired with a delightful cloche bucket hat and holding a foil pan lined with cupcakes, Jane soared into the offices of Hagger, Hagger and Miller. Today, she meant business.

Thanks to her last visit here, when she'd met with Tony to discuss the other murder investigation, she knew the receptionist possessed a sweet tooth.

As she strode deeper into the room, purse swinging at her side, she scanned the fourth story of the most exclusive office building in town. Nothing had changed. Shiny walnut walls, white marble floors and ceiling high bookshelves stuffed with rows of law books. Not one fun thing. Not even a plant.

A reception counter formed a large half circle up ahead, a candle burning on each end, filling the air with the scent of cranberry-vanilla cookies. She breathed deep. As a nod to the fall season, a cluster of wicker pumpkins dominated the counter's center.

The thin-lipped Mrs. Sharon Butterfield commanded the area. She'd slicked her graying hair into a tight bun. Not a single flyaway strand in sight.

Jane approached with a smile and placed the pan between them. "Hello, Ms. Butterfield. I did some baking this morning and thought you might enjoy my maple pecan cupcakes with a powered sugar glaze. Here's a dozen."

A phone rang. Ms. Butterfield glanced up from her typing. Frowning, she held up an index finger, then picked up the receiver. "Hagger, Hagger and Miller," she said with zero inflection of emotion. She also set the gift next to her keyboard and peeked under the lid.

The matron had been equally cool in the past, when Jane had visited Tony. But no matter. She expected to win the woman over at some point.

Mrs. Butterfield engaged in a short, choppy conversation, then hung up and motioned to the door at her left. "Go on back, Miss Ladling. End of the hall. Mr. Hagger is expecting you."

"Thank you. And Mrs. Butterfield? I'm really sorry about your loss." Whether or not the receptionist had liked Tony didn't matter. One of her bosses had been murdered. A travesty any way you sliced it.

"Oh. Yes. Well." A bit flustered now, the older woman patted her hair. "He's certainly missed. By some of us, anyway." She pushed the final words through clenched teeth.

Ohhhh. Had that been a crack directed at Hagger? Talk about fuel for Jane's fire!

Readier than ever, she skirted around the counter and strode through the door. She passed Tony's office—closed, dang it, preventing a walk-by peek-in—and entered the one at the end of the hall, as directed. Oh wow. Triple the size of Tony's and maybe even bigger than Jane's entire cottage.

Hagger sat behind a large, ornate desk with a panoramic wall of windows as his backdrop. Those windows overlooked the delightful pond separating this building from the historic Manor on Prospect Street, the most exclusive B&B in town. Plaques dictating his accomplishments peppered the walls. Baseball memorabilia filled a display case.

"Have a seat," he said, a clear command. Even without a costume, he was more imposing in person than in video. Forget the thinning hair and rotund center. A haughty expression and expensive suit granted him an air of authority.

Though everything about his demeanor chaffed, she offered him a sunny smile. He'd agreed to see her free of charge. Best not to push. "Thank you. Don't mind if I do." She smoothed the dress's skirt and settled into a soft, padded chair in front of his elaborate desk.

He studied her as he stroked the barrel of a designer fountain pen. "I know all about you and your sleuthing, Miss Ladling. Tony had much to say about it when he worked your case."

"Oh? Please, do tell," she invited, knowing Hagger wanted the words to hang above her head like an executioner's sword.

"I believe his description included the phrases *overly curious, questionably obtuse* and *annoyingly innocent*."

"Well. How kind of him," she said. Honestly, the person he'd just described sounded pretty amazing to Jane.

He revealed the barest hint of a sneer. "For once, I think he got it right."

"Not his biggest fan, I see."

A vein bulged in his brow. He might kick her out sooner

rather than later. "What is it you wish to know, Miss Ladling?"

"Give me a sec." No time to waste. She withdrew her notebook and a pen—an ordinary ballpoint that cost less than a dollar. "I already know Tony lost a lot of clients after his divorce. Maybe even before. You couldn't have wanted to continue partnering with him. Is that why the two of you argued at the party?"

Rather than react with any kind of human emotion, he schooled his expression. Inscrutable, level five. "I do not confirm or deny that we argued. But if we did, the topic of discussion is none of your business."

"Oh, no worries." She waved a hand through the air. "I don't need you to confirm or deny anything. I have the argument on video." If only that video had come with sound. "So does GBH. But I have to wonder. Why did you agree to meet with me if you planned to evade my questions?"

His eyelids narrowed to tiny slits, downgrading his poker face to level two. "To tell you this. Instead of trying to pin the murder on me, you should be investigating Emma Miller's boyfriend."

"Come again?" Emma had a full-on boyfriend? She'd mentioned dating around, but nothing about a possible relationship.

Hagger leaned forward and tossed a folder at Jane. "Before the divorce was finalized, Tony paid a PI to follow her. The guy snagged some interesting images, don't you think?"

As she flipped through an assortment of photos, she struggled not to gape. Goatee! The wiry guy from the video, who'd followed Emma at the party. He and the nurse had done an awful lot of PDA. In front of a movie theater. Outside the clinic, propped against an old sports car. On a porch swing.

Had Conrad seen these?

"Meet Reggie Belfry," Hagger said. "Some wannabe chef from Atlanta trying to make a name for himself with an internet show. The two met when he came to Aurelian Hills to film a segment about small town diners."

So much information. And the attorney couldn't dish it fast enough, could he? As if he was doing everything in his power to throw suspicion off himself. But, to his credit, Emma did look guilty as heck. Jane could think of only one reason for the nurse to hide the seriousness of her association with the chef. And from her own private investigator, no less, who she'd offered to pay "whatever you want." Emma and her boyfriend had planned and executed the murder together.

Or, maybe Mr. Belfry had done it on his own as a romantic gesture of sorts, all *Tada! I got rid of your ex for you. Marry me*. Did Emma hope to protect him now?

Hagger tilted back in his chair and linked his fingers over his middle. "I've given you enough of my valuable time, Miss Ladling. Unless you want to pay my hourly rate, you need to leave."

"No worries. I'm happy to go," she said, returning her notebook to her purse and standing. Though she'd only gotten to ask one question on her list of thirty, she had learned more than she'd hoped. In fact, she was feeling surprisingly optimistic and expected to solve this thing in record time. She'd just narrowed her list down to three. Emma, Hagger and this Belfry. Plus the doctors. So, more of a solidifying than a narrowing. But honestly, investigative work really was a piece of cake. Not to toot her own horn, but... toot, toot.

"By the way. If you killed him, Mr. Hagger, I *will* find out and you *will* spend the rest of your life in prison. Okay, bye."

With a final smile and a little finger wave, she strode from his office.

As soon as Jane shut herself inside her vehicle—an honest to goodness hearse—she whipped out her phone, thinking to text Emma about her maybe-maybe-not boyfriend. Except, she teared up when she spied the screen. A text from Fiona had come in, bringing more good news about Sheriff Moore. He'd been released from the hospital earlier than expected and was now resting comfortably at home.

What a glorious day! Jane decided to surprise the couple with several bags of groceries. Things they could snack on. She'd also whip up a few of Fiona's favorite casseroles. To aid the sheriff's recovery, Jane would use half the butter, a bit less cream, and only crumbles of bacon. Yes, yes. She liked this plan. After she spoke with Emma via text, and visited with Dr. Garcia and Dr. Price in person, she'd head to the store.

Here goes. She typed up her first message, opting for finesse rather than a blatant accusation.

Jane: *Does the name Reggie Belfry mean anything to you??????*

A reply popped up only seconds later, as if the nurse had been waiting for just such a query.

Nurse Emma: *I've been on a few dates with him, but we're not serious. Why?*

Uh, did Belfry know they weren't serious? The way he'd stalked her at the party suggested no.

Another text came in.

Nurse Emma: *Wait. Do you think Reggie harmed Tony? Because he didn't. He wouldn't. He's a hothead, but he's not violent. Besides, he wasn't even at the event. I never told him about it.*

Gah! Jane exhaled with a huff. Maybe investigative work

wasn't as easy as she'd supposed. Who to believe? Hagger or Emma? The video corroborated Emma's seeming ignorance of Belfry's presence. But what if she merely sought to cover her tracks?

Maybe Belfry was the kind of guy who thought he owned a woman, just because he'd paid for a meal and received a couple kisses. Maybe he'd been jealous of Tony and killed him out of spite, without Emma's knowledge.

Bottom line? Jane needed to speak with "hothead" Reggie Belfry.

She added another task to her to do list. Hunt down Belfry. Which she'd do as soon as she got home…before her date with Conrad kicked off.

Do not think about the date. Or the agent. Her hand shook as she stabbed the hearse key into the ignition. Since Med and Care was closer to her current location, she went that way first. Only, as she meandered along Vermeil Street, admiring the fall decorations, she caught sight of Beau, coming out of The Burger Joint with a plastic sack stuffed to the brim and dangling from a hand.

Uh, this was his important task of the day? Rather than guarding the cemetery while she helped prove his innocence in an ongoing murder investigation, he'd slept in and grabbed brunch…for two?

Her mind whirled. He wasn't headed toward Prospect Street, the fancy part of town she'd just vacated. Which signified he wasn't headed for his home. A gorgeous building that also served as the office for Peach State Security. *That* indicated he wasn't feeding Isaac and Holden, who were on the clock. So, what was Beau's destination and with whom did he plan to dine?

Curiosity exploded through Jane. She whipped the hearse to the curb and parked under an oak tree with gold and red leaves, praying the vet hadn't spotted her. Surely he hadn't. His back was to her. As quickly as possible, she killed the engine, slung her purse strap across her chest, and exited.

Sticking to the shadowy part of the sidewalk, she trailed him by roughly twenty steps. When a sudden breeze blew off her hat, she didn't turn to give chase. Yet. Though she'd waited weeks for the darling sapphire headpiece to go on sale, she kept her sights glued to Beau. She'd hunt down the hat later.

The longer she followed, the more guilt prickled her skin. Should she really be doing this? Tracking her dear friend?

Well. Yeah. Absolutely. Hadn't she vowed to cross any line to find the truth? Learning Beau's secret would only help her clear his good name.

Anyone she encountered along the way, she avoided. Which wasn't difficult. *Ignored once again.*

Spotting Tiffany and Abigail at the Treasure Room, she pumped her arms and legs with great force. The two were eating scones, sipping lattes, and laughing at a small, round table outside. Thankfully, they didn't notice her. Even when her phone rang. A call she disregarded. Had to be the reporter, Ms. Katz.

Beau turned a corner, momentarily disappearing from view. Again, Jane quickened her step, snaked the same corner and—smacked into a hard wall of strength. She bounced back, catching herself before she fell.

"Want to tell me why you're on my six?" Beau asked, both pleasant and curious. So different with her than he was with others. Sunlight bathed him, highlighting every strand of glistening gold in his hair and deepening his tan.

"Not particularly, no," she replied, meeting his gaze with a distinct lack of shame. "For the record, at what point did you notice me?"

He pounded his chest with his free hand, then arched a

brow, all *girl, please*. "Bo-bo notice Janie when she hit Vermeil."

She snorted at his expert caveman impersonation. "Janie will work on her stealth. In the meantime, would you like me to give you an update on your case?"

Two twenty-something women holding shopping bags skirted around them, rubbernecking to keep their gazes locked on Beau. He didn't seem to notice.

"Silly question," Jane said, motoring on. "Of course you do. Who wouldn't? I'll fill you in as we walk." She wouldn't stop talking until they reached his destination. "Well? What are you waiting for? Come on."

With a roll of his eyes, he started forward. Happy as a clam, Jane strolled at his side, telling him about everything she'd learned and everyone she'd spoken with. Then she shared each of her suspicions. By the end, those green irises of his possessed a wee bit of a glaze.

"The way your mind works," he said, and he even sounded dazed. Conrad often used the same tone paired with the same look. Must be a guy thing.

"I can rule out Lucy Chang," Beau added. "Holden bumped into her soon after Fiona's scream. He started running toward the noise at go."

Wait. Hold up. "Where did this bump in occur?"

"Eden Valley, near the bridge. Or on the bridge. I'm not sure. Yes, she had time to kill Tony and sprint hard from the Valley of Dolls, but she wasn't winded, so it isn't likely."

So Lucy legit wanted to hire Jane? Not to influence the outcome of the investigation, but to take advantage of her extraordinary talents? Well. Pride puffed her chest. She lifted her chin and thrust back her shoulders. What an interesting development.

Unless Lucy had hired an assassin? Because why hadn't the loan officer mentioned the encounter?

"How does Holden even know who Lucy is?" she asked. "It was dark, and he was in a hurry, yes? I doubt he lingered."

Another *girl, please* expression was cast her way. "First, Peach State Security didn't let anyone operate a booth without doing a checkup. We knew every name and face. Second, we work best in the dark."

Well. Talk about a perfect meet cute! Except. Again, Lucy hadn't mentioned a bump in the Viking-like warrior. Something anyone with a pulse would remember. Plus, such a detail helped clear her name. Assuming the assassin thing didn't pan out. But why not shout about Holden from the rooftop? Unless she didn't want Jane to know she'd ventured into Eden Valley? Why go into the unlit Eden Valley in the first place? Only one reason made sense. Lucy acted as the murderer's lookout.

Hey! Jane frowned, realizing she and Beau were back on Vermeil Street. They'd stopped next to her car, which she'd parked beside a pole with a flier advertising a Halloween party at Tiffany Hotchkins's house. Big, bold letters proclaimed, "NO ONE WILL DIE." Considering the events of the past few months—and Tiffany's entanglements in them—the widow might be making a promise she couldn't keep.

Jane humphed. "I think we're walking in circles."

Her companion faced her, giving her a genuine smile she loved to see. "This is where we part."

Oh. Darn him! Was there any better secret keeper in Aurelian Hills than Mr. Beauregard Harden?

With a heavy sigh, she hugged him, careful not to disturb the bag of food. "I hope you have a wonderful day, even though you are currently the most irritating man in the world."

"I consider that high praise," he said as she climbed into the hearse. "I'll see you tomorrow."

Jane made the drive to Med and Care, only to find an empty parking lot. Closed? Why?

She drove to the other clinic, but both Dr. Garcia and Emma were out to lunch. Together?

Frustrated, Jane journeyed to the store to get those groceries for Fiona and the sheriff. Afterward, she would go home, bake, check out Reggie Belfry, and read through Lucy's correspondence with Tony. The loan officer might not have committed the murder herself, but there was still a chance she'd worked with a partner. Perhaps someone she'd mentioned to the lawyer.

This was a better plan anyway, Jane decided. She would question the physicians tomorrow, armed with new information. After all, Conrad had promised to share what he'd learned from the doctors during their interviews with Agent Hightower.

Her heart thumped against her ribs. Conrad. Their date. A night that would end with raging success or unmitigated disaster.

CHAPTER EIGHT

"Hot off the press. Your only competition is yourself."
Ashley Katz, The Headliner

At 7:00 p.m. sharp, a hard double knock sounded at Jane's door. Eek! Conrad was here.

She hadn't yet chosen a hat. Nothing matched her bright blue and white dress with half sleeves and a flowing skirt. She shouldn't have spent so much time watching internet videos of Reggie Belfry, but each one had been more fascinating than the last, providing insight into his character.

He was definitely capable of murder. Impulsive. Someone who made lightning-fast, last-minute decisions to use incompatible ingredients. Unwilling to tolerate a single question from those there to help him. A risk-taker who thought of himself as a ladies' man. How many times had he purred his words and winked at his audience after dishing some wild innuendo? Any errors he'd blamed on his sous chef.

"Behave while Momma is out with Conrad, all right," she told Rolex, who stretched out on the bed amid the myriad of outfits she'd tried on and discarded. "Don't worry. I'm not going to fall for him."

His paw pointed to a headband with a small white bow on the side.

Oh! How perfect. "Thank you, darling." Stomach in knots, she anchored the headband in place, then made her way to the front door. Her hand trembled as she turned the knob...

And there he was. The city boy slash fairy tale prince of her dreams and nightmares.

He stood on the porch, framed in fading sunlight, a golden halo seeming to shine above his dark hair. The perfect contrast for the determined gleam in his amber eyes. He'd shaved, yet she detected a shadow of scruff on his strong jaw. A charcoal gray suit fit his broad shoulders and muscular build in the best way.

He absolutely stole her breath. Even better—and worse—he held the most amazing funeral arrangement she'd ever seen. An array of pink, purple and red roses, carnations, and mums, mixed with lighter accent flowers and lush green foliage.

Voice a bit rough, he said, "You are exquisite, Jane."

A flush burned her cheeks. "Thank you. And you are...all mine. No!" she rushed to correct, even as she imagined dropping into a six-foot hole. "I mean, you are beautiful. No, I mean, you are handsome. A real grade A beefcake. Yes, that's the phrase I was searching for."

"I liked your first description best." He winked and unveiled a genuine smile. "Are you nervous, sweetheart? Don't be. I won't bite. Unless you ask real nice." As she floundered for a response, he laughed and offered her the flowers. "These are for you."

"Thank you," she repeated, clutching the bouquet to her chest. "Come in while I gather my things."

After placing the colorful arrangement in Grandma Lily's

prized crystal vase, Jane displayed the masterpiece on the mantel. Rolex watched her from the couch. He perched at the top, gargoyle style.

She skipped over to give him a scratch behind the ears. More interested in their guest, he leaned to the side to peek around her.

"Remember what we discussed, young man." Jane padded to her bedroom and snatched up her purse. Her phone rang. Ugh. It was the reporter again, wasn't it?

Yep. Sure enough. To ensure the woman didn't bug her the rest of the night, Jane answered with a firm, "This is Miss Ladling." Someone pat her on the back, because dang. She'd never sounded more professional.

"About time," the journalist muttered. Then at a louder volume, she said, "Hello. My name is Ashley Katz, and I'm with the Headliner. If you have a few minutes, I'd love to talk with you about—"

"I don't have a few minutes," Jane interjected. "I don't even have a few seconds."

Far from deterred, the reporter asked, "Are you sure? Because rumors are already circulating. Several people in town think you paid your friends to kill Anthony Miller in order to spice up your party."

Well. As far as motives went, that wasn't bad. "What about the rumors suggesting *your* involvement, Ms. Katz? I heard you might have committed the heinous crime to give yourself a story." Truth. Jane had heard it all right…in her own mind. Just now. And honestly? It made all kinds of sense. The woman's persistence screamed *On the hunt for a cover-up.*

After sputtering a bit, the reporter hung up. Jane decided to pay her new nemesis a visit very soon and confront her about her potential involvement directly.

Satisfied with a job well done, she double checked the position of her headband, then rejoined Conrad in the living room. He waited by the door, his expression softening as she approached.

When he wound his arm around her waist and escorted her outside, her heart thumped all over again. Warmth radiated from him, chasing away the evening chill. She waved to Rolex before shutting and locking the door.

Conrad helped her into his sedan. Soon, they were on the road, headed to…the city? Oh goodness gracious. A solid hour in a small space, breathing in his incredible scent? Would she survive? Already her thoughts were growing foggy, making her forget all the reasons being with him was a terrible idea.

"Where, um, are we going?" she asked.

Amusement played at the corner of his mouth. He looked so confident behind the wheel of a car, so at ease. "You'll see."

"You seriously won't tell me?"

"I seriously won't." He reached over and linked their fingers, resting their joined hands against the top of her thigh. "I know how much you enjoy mysteries."

I will not fall for this man. At last, the reasons surged to the forefront of her mind. She had rules, remember? Very strict rules. The strictest! "Tell me another horrible fact about yourself right this second. A truth worse than the toilet paper thing if possible. Make it something sure to color my perception of you for the rest of eternity."

"No problem." He gave her hand a little squeeze. "I've been saving this one for a high danger moment. Are you sure you're ready for it, though?"

Realizing she was clinging to him, she nodded. "Beyond ready. Horrify me."

"Here goes." He brought her hand to his mouth and kissed her knuckles. Wait. Did she detect a slight tremor? Her jaw went slack. What the heck did he plan to tell her? "I—nope. I won't tell you this, either." A shake of his head. "You think you're ready, but you're not."

"Oh! You little tease!" He'd done that on purpose. "You got me all excited for nothing."

"Don't worry, sweetheart." His voice dipped. "Before the night is over, I'll excite you again. It's my mission."

JANE REMAINED dazed and breathless for the rest of the drive, still clinging to Conrad's hand. When he stopped in the lot of a well-lit city park, she scanned the area with unsurpassed curiosity. Trees showed off an array of fall colors. A wealth of orange, red and gold. Old-fashioned streetlights mixed with small glowing bulbs lined cobblestone paths. But…why here?

"This is Loblolly Park," he explained. "I used to picnic here with my family. Before."

He didn't fill in the rest, but then, he didn't need to. Before. The time a car accident killed his parents and younger brother, sending Conrad into a succession of different foster homes and facilities.

Without thinking things through, she brought Conrad's hand to her mouth and kissed *his* knuckles. A gesture of comfort and empathy.

She lifted her head, and he used his other hand to trace the pad of his thumb along the outline of her lips. A gasp escaped her, and she released him. He didn't pull back. He glided his fingers over her jawline and hooked a lock of hair behind her ear. Tremors rocked her.

"C'mon." Taking pity on her, he reached for a large wicker basket stowed in the back seat. "We've got a little hike ahead of us."

A picnic? Oh, how delightful!

He exited into the moonlight, then strode around to open her car door. After helping her out, he led her along the light-lined path. Walking trails fanned off in several directions. How often had young Conrad run and laughed and played here? They passed a pavilion, a massive playground and a gorgeous two-tiered fountain. Crystal blue water poured over a basin filled with shiny coins.

"Did you ever make a wish?" she asked.

"Once or twice."

"And what did young Conrad wish for back then, hmm?"

"The usual. Superpowers. And for no one, anywhere, to call me Connie. The name my brother used whenever he teased me." Affection thickened his voice. "Did little Jane make any wishes?"

"She did indeed. More funerals. I loved helping Pops and Grandma Lily tend to the mourners and ensure each gravesite looked its best."

He snickered. "That is the most Jane thing I've ever heard."

They reached an open, moonlit stretch of grass, where another couple picnicked. Jane helped him spread a checkered red and white blanket, and they eased down, side by side.

The wicker creaked as he lifted the basket's top. He pulled out a single lily, and Jane nearly teared up. A bloom meant to honor her grandmother?

"I got the food from Daisy's," he said, placing the flower on her lap. The backs of his knuckles grazed the bare skin above her knee, igniting a spear of fire.

Ignore your shivers. "I adore Daisy's. There's nothing her chicken noodle soup can't cure."

He winked at her. "So you've told me."

Oh yes. Soon after they'd first met, Jane had contracted

the world's worst cold. In a medicated haze, she'd called the special agent dozens of times, saying the most humiliating things and begging for Daisy's no-fail elixir.

Next, he withdrew two wrapped sandwiches. Daisy's famous chicken salad on freshly baked sweet bread. Jane could almost taste the vine-ripened tomatoes. Wait. She sniffed the air. Did she detect the salty aroma of chips?

Her jaw dropped. "You didn't."

"Didn't what?" he asked, puzzled.

"You snagged Daisy's artisan potato chips? She handmakes those babies each morning. People stand in line to buy a bag. Which is why she's always out by ten. I've only managed to score them on three occasions—days I still celebrate each year."

He gifted her with his lopsided smile. Her favorite one. A real sense destroyer. "I may have Daisy's private number and permission to call anytime I have an order."

What! "How?" Jane demanded. No one had Daisy's private number. Maybe not even Daisy herself!

"Dr. Hotchkins was her cousin, and she wanted to thank me for finding his killer."

"Uh, *I* found the killer. And I live in town. We're neighbors. Kind of." But dang it! How could Jane have forgotten about the familial connection?

His smile widened, as if such a detail were unimportant. "When I called and explained I was planning a special date for the infamous Jane Ladling, she told me she'd handle it."

Special date. With her. Warmth spread in her chest.

He finished off the meal prep by pouring peach tea into wine glasses that had been nestled in the lid of the picnic basket.

"Thank you. For everything," she said. "This is truly wonderful."

"I'm glad you like it." He opened his bag of chips. "Gotta admit, I'm eager to try one of these now."

"Prepare for transport to Heaven." She stole one and popped it into her mouth before he could protest. Magnificent taste bombs burst on her tongue, and she moaned.

He watched her, his whisky eyes darkening. Then he sampled a chip—and shrugged. "Not bad."

Not bad? Not bad! She snatched the bag from him. "You don't deserve these!"

He snatched it back and mock growled, "Mine."

"All right. Now that's more like it." And thank goodness. Otherwise she'd have to question his intelligence. But either way, this was already, hands down, the single best night of Jane's entire life.

Oh no! That thought. Danger, danger! *Won't fall for him. Absolutely, positively will not.*

"Um, you promised me some information," she reminded him. Yes. Focus on the case rather than the delightful picnic he'd planned. "Which, I admit, surprised me. I mean, you said insisting I keep my brilliance out of your work did you no good, but what a shocking turn around."

"I did promise, and I was insistent before, yes. I'm trying something new." Conrad shifted in his seat, now in full-on agent of the law mode. "I can't tell you everything. But. You may ask me questions, and we'll go from there."

Meaning, she could ask, but he might not answer? "Let's get started then. So which came first, the drug or the beating?"

"Which do you think?"

"The beating?" Tony had been universally disliked, so there was a good chance the killer wanted him to hurt before dying.

Conrad bopped the tip of her nose. "Guess who won her honorary detective's badge?"

She'd gotten it right? Jane fluffed her hair. "Well. That isn't a surprise. I'm not just a cutie, Officer Inspector Detective Special Agent Ryan. I'm a smarty, too."

"That you are. But when did I become an inspector on top of everything else?"

"Today. I gave you a promotion in my mind." Okay, on to the next question, before he charmed her silly. "Did GBH find fingerprints on the syringe? Other than Fiona's. I'm guessing no."

"Then you've lost your brand-new detective's badge."

Well, drats. But whose fingerprints had they found? "If there are fingerprints, why hasn't an arrest been made?"

"That, you'll have to answer on your own."

Jane popped another chip into her mouth and washed it down with peach tea while racking her brain. Many of her guests had worn gloves to ward off the night's chill. Wait. Had the prints belonged to Tony himself? Had he been conscious after his strike to the head? Had he fought his attacker?

"My turn to ask *you* a question," he said. "Other than Emma, are you still considering a certain medical professional as a top suspect?"

"I am. At the party, Dr. Price did an awful lot of slinking through the darkness." Before she asked her next question, she took Conrad's earlier advice and batted her baby blues at him. "Do *you* still consider Dr. Price a suspect?"

He moaned and said, "I can tell you he isn't a person of interest at this time."

Oh. Hmm. Well. Poor Conrad and his by the book investigating. He missed so much. "What about Dr. Garcia?"

"This is public knowledge currently posted on the Headliner, so I'm free to share. Some of your guests claimed he fell ill. That he was searching for a bathroom he couldn't find when Fiona screamed."

"Wait." Jane paused with the sandwich halfway to her mouth. "Are you telling me he used my bushes to…?"

"No. He told us his stomach calmed before it came to that."

"Oh, thank goodness." But also super convenient. And majorly suspicious! Garcia had just offered such embarrassing information to anyone who would listen? Up the list he went, earning a top spot beside Emma, Hagger and Belfry. "So, uh–"

Conrad's phone rang, interrupting her. He grimaced as he slid the device out of his pocket. "I've got to take this. My cell is on 'do not disturb' for every number but Hightower's. We've been waiting for a specific bit of information."

"I understand." And what a wonderful opportunity to listen in! "Go ahead." *Please.*

He snorted, as if reading her mind, then brought the phone to his ear. "Ryan." A pause as he listened. "Too bad. I'm on a date." More talking from Hightower, followed by a heavy sigh from Conrad. "I'm either twenty minutes or two hours away, depending on whether or not I drive my girlfriend home. Which do you prefer?"

Girlfriend. New, stronger tremors shook Jane, these born of disappointment. The single best night of her life was about to end abruptly, wasn't it?

No help for it. The case came first. She gathered the leftovers, stacking them in the picnic basket.

"Forget it, not happening," Conrad told Hightower. Then he nodded. "All right. Yes. That, I can do."

When he signed off, he flashed a chagrined smile at Jane. "I know your answer before I ask, but are you okay if we drop by a restaurant called Primordial?"

She sucked air between her teeth. "The one owned by Reggie Belfry?" A prime suspect as well as Emma's maybe, maybe not boyfriend? Jane popped to her feet and smoothed out her skirt. "Yes, yes, yes! My very first official stakeout."

"Second place to a murder investigation," he grumbled. "The indignity."

Oh, if only he knew.

"It's not a stakeout," he said as they returned to the car. "Not for me, anyway. It's a Q and A. You'll wait in the car."

"Of course."

They hit the road. Each mile closer to their destination, Conrad grew more serious and professional. And unfortunately, more tight-lipped as well. Finally, he drew into a lot with few cars, in front of an old, dingy building.

Guess Mr. Belfry's internet fame didn't translate to money making.

A tall woman with a straight inverted bob emerged from an already parked sedan as Conrad killed the engine. Hightower. As he reached for his door handle, Jane's phone buzzed, alerting her to a new text message.

"I'm going in to speak with Mr. Belfry," he said. "Lock up after me. And do not leave this car for any reason."

"Promise. Maybe. Probably."

"Lord save us all," he muttered. "Also, don't eat my chips."

What! He still had half a bag in the basket, while she had none. "Really?" She batted her lashes again. Why mess with a sure thing? "You won't share even one?"

He snorted. "Go ahead and have them all. It seems I can deny you nothing."

She beamed at him, and he shook his head at her, clearly fighting a grin as he exited. But his expression went blank before he turned on his heel and strode toward the other agent. Jane had to admit she enjoyed watching him walk away. A treat in itself.

Great! Time for a distraction. She grabbed her phone and read the message.

Beaudyguard: *I hacked into private conversations on the Headliner. Found out some things. GBH interviewed Dr. Frederick Price, who claimed he recognized Tony at the party. Said Tony harassed nurses at Pinetum, so P followed T just in case "the drunk tried to hurt someone." But. P lost sight of T before Fee's scream and proved it with a time-stamped live video he sent two of his staff members. I'm still working on obtaining that video.*

Well, no wonder Dr. Price had been ruled out by GBH. But was his alibi *too* tidy?

Beaudyguard: *But wait, there's more. Are you ready to have your mind blown?*

Jane: *Always!*

Her phone rang, and she smiled as Beau's number popped on the screen.

"It'll be easier to speak this particular conversation," he said without preamble. "This part, I learned another way. Don't ask me how. So get this. Tony had a knife and two burner phones in his possession. He'd used one cell to search for the best places to stab someone for the most painful death. Using a refillable gift card, he also purchased a ticket to the party under the name Chris P. Bacon, which GBH believes he mailed to Reggie Belfry in secret. Belfry was never able to confirm who sent it to him. With the second cell, Tony bought an additional ticket under the name Al Dente. Mailed in a different envelope on a different day. Which doesn't make sense. Why use two phones? Why buy two tickets for one person?"

"Good gracious." So much to absorb. She *did* remember seeing Dente on the guest list, just like Bacon. While the first had struck her as odd, the second had soared right past her. But hearing the name spoken aloud...super odd. "Do you think Tony planned to kill Belfry, the man dating his ex-wife? Maybe he sent the second ticket to double the chances of tempting the chef to attend?"

"He might have planned to kill Emma and blame Belfry."

"Or he hoped to kill them both." Whatever he'd set out to do, someone had gotten to him first.

What if Tony attacked Belfry, but the chef fought back and killed the attorney instead? Then, Belfry heard Fiona's approach, panicked and fled the scene. A scenario that made tons of sense. But why not stick around to prove he'd acted in self-defense? Fear?

Fear *did* make people do foolish things.

"I can tell your mind is racing in a million different directions," Beau said. "Let's talk again tomorrow."

"Tomorrow," she echoed, and they hung up. What did Conrad think of all this?

Her gaze flipped up. He and Hightower hadn't yet entered the restaurant. They stood together, discussing something.

Jane waved when the female agent glanced over, but she was ignored. Still irritated because a cemetery owner had solved the last two cases? Yeah, that tracked.

Finally the agents headed inside. With Beau's info front and center, she grew desperate to listen to Belfry's informal—formal?—questioning. What if the chef worked to frame Fiona and Beau even now? How could Jane *not* listen?

Staring at the entrance, she ran through her options. Call in a to-go order on the off chance she'd overhear their conversation in the background? No. The likelihood of success was too low. But there was only one other route to choose...

Guilt pooled in Jane's stomach as she opened a specific app on her phone. The one she and Conrad had downloaded during the second murder investigation...the one he and Beau had used to listen to her conversations at the party. It allowed them to activate her cell's microphone...and Jane to activate theirs.

Beau had probably already uninstalled it. But Jane hadn't. And she'd bet Conrad hadn't, either. *Taking advantage...*

Wait. He was a smart, observant man. If he hadn't expected her to listen to this interrogation, he would've taken measures to stop her, right? Honestly, it was almost like he *wanted* her to do it.

After only a slight hesitation, she tapped the proper button.

"–get you fired," Hightower was muttering.

Bingo!

"She's not up for discussion," he all but growled.

She. As in Jane? A heavy weight fell over her. *Would* she get Conrad fired?

The two agents went quiet as the sound of clanging pots and pans intensified. Then someone shouted, "If I had a better sous chef, I'd have customers!"

"Reggie Belfry?" Hightower announced. "I'm Special Agent Hightower, and this is Special Agent Ryan. We'd like to ask you a few questions regarding the death of Anthony Miller." She paused. "No, don't run. It'll only make things worse for you." A weary sigh crackled from the phone. "And he's running."

More banging pots and pans. Pounding footsteps. Shuffling and rustling. Grunts. Clinking metal. "Reggie Belfry, you are under arrest."

Oh, wow. Conrad had chased him down and was now cuffing him!

"What for?" Reggie demanded. "I was taking a stroll. A man is allowed to walk."

"You fled the scene to evade an officer of the law. You also obstructed justice by knowingly hindering an investigation. Shall I go on?" Hightower asked.

Conrad began a very familiar spiel. "You have the right to remain silent. Anything–"

"I didn't kill him," the chef shouted.

"–you say can and will be used against you in a court of law. You have a right to an attorney. If you cannot afford an attorney, one will be appointed for you."

"I wasn't even gonna attend that stupid party until I found out Emma was going with her ex," Reggie spat.

Stupid? How dare he!

More shuffling and grunts. Minutes later, Hightower, Conrad and the shackled Belfry were striding out of the building. As Conrad ensured the suspect was secured inside Hightower's vehicle, Jane closed the app and stored her phone. The two agents spoke before he returned to the car.

The second he was seated behind the wheel, the guilt overwhelmed her and she blurted out, "I did it! I used the phone app to listen in. And honestly, it wasn't even worth it because you didn't have a chance to interrogate the suspect."

He peered at her, silent for a long while, before shaking his head. "I can't believe anyone ever suspected *you* of murder. You would make the worst criminal."

Wait. That was it? That was all he had to say? "Conrad, I betrayed your trust in the most heinous way. Yell at me. Break up with me. Something!"

"Jane," he said, putting the car in reverse. "Stop being adorable. We have an hour-long drive ahead of us, and I'm determined to remain a gentleman."

Adorable? So he *had* expected her to do it? Because he'd wanted their first date to be special for her, and he just couldn't admit it?

Great! Her guilt worsened ten thousand degrees. What if she truly did get him fired?

Wringing her hands, wondering if she should end things now, before she caused any more problems, she asked, "Does this mean we aren't following Hightower and listening in as she grills Belfry for the truth, the whole truth and nothing but the truth?"

He snorted. "We most certainly are not doing that. And I told you to stop being adorable."

Won't fall for a city boy.

Once again, he reached over to link his fingers with hers.

Nope, I won't do it.

They didn't speak again until he escorted her to the cottage door. The porch light glowed all around them.

"Well," she rasped. Should she invite him in? Shouldn't she?

"Well," he echoed. With his chin down and his eyes locked on her, he backed her against the door. His big, calloused hands cupped her jaw. He brushed his thumbs over the rise of her cheeks. "Don't invite me in," he told her, as if reading her mind. "I'll say yes, and I shouldn't."

Heart thundering in her chest, she licked her lips. "Why shouldn't you?"

"If you're questioning whether to do it or not, you're not ready. And I can wait. I'm happy to wait. Until then..." He lowered his head and kissed her.

Oh, did he kiss her. Jane could do nothing but cling and kiss him back.

Okay, so, I might be falling for him.

CHAPTER NINE

"Victory comes with an up-front cost, yes, but defeat comes with a high interest rate."
Lucy Chang, loan officer

Bang, bang, bang.

No! No, no, no. Not again. Groaning, Jane blinked open an eye to glance at the clock on her phone. 3:53 a.m. Ugh. One hour and seven minutes until her alarm went off. What's more, multiple texts awaited her review. The first three came from Conrad.

Hello. Talk about an instant wake up. She jolted upright, the intruder forgotten. What did the special agent have to say? Something about their explosive end of date kiss?

Bang, bang, bang.

Another groan escaped her. Intruder remembered. "Why me?" Jane asked the ceiling. "What did I do to deserve another morning visitor who prevents me from reading my boyfriend's correspondence?"

Bang, bang, gang.

"Hold your horses," she muttered, tossing the phone aside

and climbing from the bed. Donning her robe, she padded into the living room. Who would it be this time?

Rolex jumped from the mattress to follow and guard her. Such a good kitty.

"Jane! Jane! It's Lucy. Lucy Chang." The loan officer's frantic voice filled the foyer.

Concern quickened her step. Jane opened up, and Lucy burst inside the cottage, bringing a chilly breeze with her. A big overnight bag hung over her shoulder. No, not a bag, after all, but a pretty pink and white cat carrier.

"Shut the door, shut the door!" Lucy commanded.

"What's going on?" she demanded as she obeyed. "Are you in danger?"

"Yes! Oliver tried to sneak into my house only an hour ago!"

"Your ex-boyfriend?" Jane asked, doing her best to connect the dots while still half asleep.

The other woman nodded. "He planned to steal Cartier, I know it. I can't let him have her again, Jane, I just can't." The words rushed from her, tinged with panic. "He doesn't even like her. And he certainly doesn't feed her the right food. Doesn't care that the cheap stuff irritates her digestive tract. He doesn't even give her the pets she so richly deserves. Nope, he only wants to punish me for breaking up with him, because that's the kind of guy he is. You've got to keep her for me. Just for a little while. Just until I know it's safe."

Choking sounds left Jane. She needed to process a probable cat nabbing without a drop of caffeine in her system?

Lucy set the carrier on the floor and scrubbed a hand over her face, upset radiating from her every pore. "I'm sorry. We barely know each other, and here I am, requesting you protect the love of my life. I just... I wasn't sure what else to do. And I knew how much you love cats."

Rolex prowled around the carrier, sniffing the mesh sides. When he pawed at the zipper, Cartier hissed.

"Don't worry. We'll figure this out. So get comfortable," Jane said, giving her guest a little nudge toward the couch. "You stay here while the cats introduce themselves, and I'll brew up some caramel apple coffee." A new blend she was excited to try.

"Yes. Okay." Relief poured from the other woman. "Thank you."

Jane popped into her bedroom to collect her phone before entering the kitchen. As the sweet smelling ambrosia brewed, she checked the messages from Conrad at long last.

Agent Spice: *Good morning, sweetheart. I haven't stopped thinking about you.*

Her heart fluttered. Thanks to this amazing man, she'd tossed and turned most of the night.

Agent Spice: *Because I know you're curious, I'll tell you Belfry is behind bars. For now. Bail hearing is later today. Circumstantial evidence is stacking up, but there's not yet enough to arrest him for murder. Probably only a matter of time. Fiona and Beau can rest easy.*

Hmm. Jane wasn't convinced Reggie Belfry did the crime. Yes, he topped her list of suspects. But so did others. Her gut told her there were new dramas and depths to be plumbed here. Of course, Jane's gut might be compromised. Last night, she'd let herself think, briefly, that she was falling for a city boy. The sheer lunacy of such a notion!

Agent Spice: *One last thing. Since we both know you're spooked and going to put me on ice for the next few days, I might as well confess. I miss you already.*

Her breath caught. He missed her…and she missed him.

City boy, city boy, city boy.

And okay, yes, Jane was indeed tempted to sink back into old habits and push Conrad away for a bit. Possibly a few weeks. Or months. Maybe a year. Anything to dampen this terrible, wonderful rush of feelings. But in the end, she strapped on her big girl panties and responded.

Jane: *I've pondered your existence periodically, I guess.*

Now then. Enough mushy gushy talk for the moment. Moving on to her other messages.

Fionality: *Thank you for the casseroles and snacks, hon. Raymond and I appreciate your thoughtfulness so much. He says your croissant and berries cream cheese casserole might snatch the first place ribbon from my famous blueberry pancakes, and I might have to agree! By the way, he's feeling better than ever!*

Jane: *That makes me so happy!!*

Next.

Nurse Emma: *I just found out Tony planned to kill me and probably Reggie too, but Reggie beat him to it. Guess my former date was involved, after all. Case closed. I don't need your services anymore.*

Wait. Had she fired Jane before a legit arrest had been made? Wow. Just wow. And no mention of setting up that playdate for their pets. Where was the integrity?

No integrity, no loyalty. No loyalty, no reason not to commit murder.

Jane would absolutely be digging deeper into Emma's story...after she questioned Lucy, spoke with Dr. Garcia and interviewed some of the party attendees. Fired or not, the case must go on. If she had time, she'd even stop by the Headliner offices to speak with the pushy Ashley Katz in person. Maybe the woman had killed for a story, maybe she hadn't. Time would tell. Either way, the texts and calls would finally end.

With two steaming mugs of coffee in hand, Jane rejoined Lucy in the living room. The loan officer sat on the couch. Cartier was out of the carrier and perched on the mantel, staring down at Rolex, who remained on the floor, peering up at her. The feline version of Romeo and Juliet.

Smiling, Jane handed Lucy one of the mugs, then eased onto the other side of the couch. "First, I'm happy to keep Cartier for you." Now that she'd seen the two cats together, how could she deny them their blooming romance? "Second, it seems like the authorities consider Reggie Belfry, Emma Miller's ex-date, the killer. He was arrested last night. Not for the murder, but GBH is working to gather evidence pointing to his guilt. I think they're wrong, but you can feel free to fire me if—"

"Fire you?" Lucy waved a hand in dismissal. She sipped the coffee and made a little mmm noise of approval. "If you think they're wrong, I think they're wrong. Oh! Speaking of the case—" She rifled through an oversize purse and withdrew some papers. "This is an outline of my activities during the party."

Hmm. Her unwavering enthusiasm was just as suspicious as Emma's indifference. What if Lucy knew Belfry wasn't responsible for the murder…because she was? On the other hand, Lucy had tasted—and liked—the coffee. She probably possessed a heart of gold.

Jane accepted the pages and skimmed the text until she reached Lucy's abandonment of her booth. Well. The loan officer claimed she'd gone on a walk to stretch her leg. No mention of Eden Valley, the bridge or the run-in with Holden.

"Were you able to open the file containing my correspondence with Tony?" Lucy asked.

"Yes, thank you." While baking those cupcakes for Ms. Butterfield and the casseroles for Fiona and the sheriff, Jane had scoured every message between Tony and his client. Nothing odd had struck her, which had struck her as odd.

"So?" Leaning closer, unblinking, the other woman asked, "Who do you think killed him?"

Was she, perhaps, too curious? "I have several persons of interest. Some of which I'll be visiting later today." Jane kept her answer deliberately vague.

"Oh!" Lucy bounced in her seat. "Can I go with you? Please? I left my boss a message, letting him know I'm taking today off. Helping you clear my name is exactly what I need to make this day brighter."

Jane almost refused. She worked best alone. Except when Beau helped. Or Fiona tagged along. Or Conrad left her crumbs of information. But why not invite her companion to join her, anyway? What better opportunity to secretly observe the loan officer's behavior with other suspects?

"All right," Jane said with a nod. "We'll lock Cartier in my bedroom and give the cats a chance to sniff each other through the crack in the door to get to know each other better while we speak with our first batter, Dr. Garcia."

WITHIN MINUTES of checking into the clinic for a walk-in appointment, Jane and Lucy were escorted out of the empty waiting room, down a hallway, and into an exam room. By Emma herself.

Jane suppressed a shudder while adjusting her straw hat. The last time she'd been in this building, PA Caroline Whittington had almost given her a permanent dirt nap.

"What are you two doing, coming here?" Emma demanded as soon as they were shut up in an exam room. Furrows etched her brow, and her jaw jutted forward. She hated that they were here? Interesting.

"We came to see—" Jane began, but the door opened back up and Dr. Garcia strode inside.

A stethoscope hung over the lapels of his lab coat. His narrowed eyes really highlighted the permanent bump on the bridge of his nose. A bump she'd caused after punching him in the face a few months ago. What? He'd startled her.

He peered at his nurse, his expression strained, and motioned to the door. "I've got this, Emma. You may go."

After the nurse's reluctant departure, Dr. Garcia crossed his arms over his chest and glanced between potential patients. "Are either one of you ill?"

Jane cleared her throat. "Define ill."

Without missing a beat, Lucy said, "Does a broken heart count?"

The fact that she hadn't lied right off the bat... maybe she was innocent of murder, after all.

Dr. Garcia compressed his lips into a thin line. He'd been Jane's primary care physician for the past decade. Though, after she'd proved his assistant had killed the other doctor who worked in this very clinic, he'd pretty much avoided contact with her. Until the night of her party. Either he'd opted to put the past behind them...or he'd pretended to do so in order to kill someone at her event.

"I don't know what you've heard, but I didn't kill Tony Miller," he grated. "I was too sick."

Allegedly sick.

"And I didn't steal opioids from Pinetum Regional," he continued. "It must have been Reggie Belfry. I knew his fight with Tony was an excuse to get into the hospital. There was just something odd about their dealings."

Um... "What fight between Tony and Belfry?" Jane asked.

Dr. Garcia massaged the back of his neck. "I can't say more without violating my oath."

Which meant, what? He'd once treated Belfry at the

hospital for injuries sustained during an altercation with Tony...and he'd done it the day the opioids went missing?

Okay, so, Conrad was right, and the circumstantial evidence was stacking up. Jane remained unconvinced, however. The doctor's behavior struck her as super suspicious. Who offered up information so casually without any real prompting? Maybe he'd worked with Belfry and now the two were turning on each other.

Her best course of action was to keep Dr. Garcia talking while she asked questions wrapped up in suspicion for another suspect. "Did Emma visit Belfry during his hospital stay?" Did the nurse have a connection to the stolen drugs as well?

"She wasn't there while I was, only his lawyer," he said, grabbing a blood pressure cuff. Now that he'd imparted his maybe false, maybe true lead, he was back to business.

Lucy raised her hand like a kid in class. "Why did he need a lawyer? Did Tony threaten him with legal action?"

The doctor's mouth curled with distaste. "Yes. Though I was surprised Belfry hired Tony's partner, considering Tony's the one who punched him."

Okay, now they were getting somewhere. Talk about a solid lead! Why would Tony's business partner represent said business partner's ex-wife's current date a mere week before Tony's death? And on the same day drugs were stolen no less?

Might be time to stop by the law office of Hagger, Hagger and Miller again.

A task for the bottom of her list. With Lucy at her side, Jane would be better served speaking with some of the booth attendees to gather as much evidence against the attorney as possible. Surely someone had overheard Hagger's argument with Tony. Hopefully, someone had overheard his conversation with Belfry in the hospital, too. An orderly. Another patient. A visitor.

"I believe you're innocent, Dr. Garcia," Lucy assured him, seeming genuinely sympathetic. "Help us prove it. Did you overhear anything the two men said to each other? Because conversation isn't included in your medical oath."

"I did not," was the staunch reply. "But then, I didn't know I'd be part of another criminal investigation and every detail of the encounter would matter."

A good lesson for all of them—be more observant, always. "Well. That's enough for now. We've taken up plenty of your time. Good day, Dr. Garcia." Hoping to run into Emma again, Jane steered her companion out of the room. Nope. No sign of the nurse. Whatever. Jane would come back tomorrow, maybe, and question her without a sidekick.

"I gotta admit, that was more fun than I expected," Lucy whispered with a grin.

"That," Jane said, with a grin of her own, "was only the beginning." As they made their way outside, she linked their arms. And dang it, it felt right. They strolled along the sidewalk, toward the shops on Vermeil Street. "Pop quiz time. Did Dr. Garcia seem guilty to you? Keep in mind, there's only one correct answer." Teasing, only teasing. Kind of.

Lucy thought for a moment. "I believe I detected fear, but not guilt. Like he's secretly afraid he's been set up. I sort of wanted to hug him."

What a kind, caring response. Too caring? Jane hoped not because, well, she was maybe digging having a new friend at her side. Sharing ideas. Brainstorming. Tag teaming suspects.

"I'm more intrigued by Mr. Hagger's involvement," Lucy admitted.

Ding, ding, ding. "I'm wondering about that myself. Problem is, I've already questioned him, and it didn't turn out well. Before I take another go at him, I've got to gather more intel. How would you like to help me question party guests?"

"Seriously?" Lucy nodded with great enthusiasm. "I would love it."

"Excellent." First stop, the Treasure Room. She'd never spoken with the owner, Hannah.

They made their way over. Hannah occupied the charmingly cluttered space, which smelled of cranberries and vanilla. She held a tray of samples that featured her latest seasonal tea—Autumn Delights.

"Try one," she said.

"Don't mind if I do." Jane accepted a paper cup. The warm brew tasted of nutmeg and cinnamon and instantly made her love fall even more.

"This is incredible," Lucy exclaimed.

Okay, enough pleasantries. "I popped by to say thank you for participating in my murder mystery game...and also sorry for what happened in the midst of it." Excellent, truthful excuse and a perfect transition to the business at hand rolled into one.

"Uh-huh. Likely story." Hannah shifted from one foot to the other as she nervously smoothed a lock of graying hair into her messy bun. "I know your reputation, young lady. You're investigating Tony's death, aren't you?"

No reason to deny it. And no reason to delay the questioning. "Did you happen to overhear a fight between Tony and Mr. Hagger that night?"

"Oh, thank goodness." The shop owner pressed a hand over her heart. "You don't think it's me. Or do you?" Relief gave way to panic. "Because you shouldn't. I didn't do it."

Or did she? Jane offered her a bland expression that made no promises.

The tea making expert scowled but said, "I never saw the two men together. I only spotted Tony once, when he was glaring down at his phone." She leaned in closer and lowered her voice. "I've heard the ex is always the first suspect in cases like these. Have you considered Emma Miller?"

Had Jane considered Emma? Ha! As if she were some kind of amateur. "Do you recall seeing anything unusual at the party?" she asked, ignoring the other woman's question.

"Other than Denise Allen flirting with Tony early in the evening? No."

Ohhhh. Flirting, huh? "Please call me at Garden of Memories if you remember anything else."

Jane dragged Lucy to the Gilded Scissor where Denise Allen worked. Denise had done face-painting for the kids and handed out twenty percent off coupons to redeem at her shop. At the moment, she was busy giving Maureen Gilmore a trim.

Both women paled as Jane and her companion neared.

"I didn't kill Tony, okay?" Denise rushed out. "He told me I looked cute, and I thanked him. If you're looking for someone to blame, try every bar owner in town. I hear he owed them all a fat stack. I'm pretty sure the love of money is the root of every murder."

Jane jotted the bar theory in her notebook. Though she didn't think it needed further investigation. A dead Tony couldn't repay his bill. "Did you spy Tony and Devin Hagger together? Or overhear an argument they had?"

"Not me," Denise said, relaxing a bit. Her companion shook her head in denial, causing the stylist to cut more than she'd intended. She closed her eyes for a moment, as if praying for patience. "Not to change the subject or anything, but have you been trimming your own bangs again, Jane?"

Uh... She winced. The reason she'd begun wearing hats to begin with, so many years ago. She tugged the brim of her current headpiece lower. "I, well–"

"Maybe the person you should be investigating is yourself," sneered a familiar voice.

Jane whipped her attention to the speaker. Tall, dark-haired Robby Waynes held a cardboard drink carrier filled with four paper coffee cups tagged with the name Gold Rush Museum. His current place of employment.

The museum delivered coffee now? Good to know. But ugh. Running into the man she'd suspected of killing the previous murder victim? Not exactly her favorite cup of tea. Though, granted, the same could be said for basically anyone in town.

He smirked at her. "Rumor has it *you're* the one who killed Tony."

Jane made a scoffing sound.

Lucy scoffed right along with her. "That's a ridiculous statement. What reason would Jane possibly have for harming Anthony Miller?"

Robby hiked his shoulders and deposited the cardboard carrier near the cash register. "According to Ashley Katz, there are tons of reasons. For starters, Cemetery Girl didn't like the way he handled her legal case. And he wasn't exactly quiet about the bill she contested. What about building up the drama at that stupid mystery party and things got out of hand?"

Stupid? As Jane's mouth opened and closed, he radiated glee, thinking he'd hit some kind of target inside her heart. Then he pivoted on his heel and left. The bell over the door tinkled, but it didn't drown out his soft laughter.

Oh! That man annoyed her. "I need to have a conversation with Ms. Katz after all," she said, pushing the words through clenched teeth. Had the reporter printed another story? Had posts shown up online via the app? Might be time for a deep dive.

"If she's spouting those kinds of lies, she's not worth your effort," Lucy assured her. "She'll only make up worse scenarios."

The support caused Jane's chest to puff up. What a surprisingly amazing cohort in anti-crime—also less and less of a suspect and more and more of a, well, friend. She *liked* the loan officer. Really, really liked her.

First a boyfriend. Now a girlfriend. How had life gotten so rich with promise?

Trepidation suddenly prickled the back of her neck, as if the curse were kicking up a fuss. Uh oh. She gulped. Something terrible was going to happen soon, wasn't it?

CHAPTER TEN

"Never forget. Second place is first loser."
Tiffany Hotchkins, heiress and widow

The next morning, Jane completed initial rounds, taking notes about plots in need of tending, and returned to the cottage. In the kitchen, she set up a feeding station for Rolex and Cartier. The two acted like long lost friends, eating side by side and sneaking nibbles from the other's bowl, even though they munched on the same thing.

She snapped a few photos and filmed a few videos. No more than ten each. Perhaps closer to fifty. And okay, yes, she might have taken too many, because Rolex glared at her as if she were seriously ruining his vibe.

"You have no idea how blessed you are. The Ladling curse only affects the women in our family," she told him. The little darling could fall ears-over-paws for Miss Cartier without having to worry he'd lose her one day.

Sighing, Jane padded to the back office to key up today's headline for the Headliner. Had Ashley Katz written another article?

Is There A Grim Reaper In Aurelian Hills?

Pressing her tongue to the roof of her mouth, Jane read on. Ms. Katz rambled about the previous two murders being linked to the third, all but warning people to stay away from the Garden of Memories.

Anger heated Jane's blood. A chat with Ms. Katz shot to the second spot on her to-do list.

Once she calmed, she texted several of those breakfast photos to Lucy with the caption, "Look at our beautiful babies!"

Despite the early hour, Lucy replied right away.

Cartier's Mom: *A match made in Heaven!!!!! I'm hearing wedding bells!*

Eighteen heart emojis accompanied the words.

Cartier's Mom: *Maybe I could come over later to see them in person? And you, of course!*

Jane: *That would be lovely. How about 7? I'll whip us up something for dinner.*

She would also invite Conrad, Beau, Fiona, and Sheriff Moore. Trick, Holden, and Isaac, too. All the members of Team Truth. She could gauge Lucy's reaction to Holden and finally ask why the loan officer hadn't mentioned their run in. There must be an innocent explanation. Either that, or Jane's new friendship was soon to crash and burn.

Cartier's Mom: *See you then!!*

She leaned back in her chair behind the antique desk, thinking about her next move. The call to Hagger, item number one on her to-do list. Well, she *tried* to think. A metal filing cabinet mocked her.

You should have digitally logged my contents ages ago.

"I know," she muttered. Instead, she'd solved two murders and flirted with the like of her life. Kind of seemed like a fair trade to her.

"I'll get to you when I get to you," she promised. "Now

leave me alone. I need to focus." With a deep breath, she picked up the Garden of Memories landline and phoned the law offices of Hagger, Hagger, and Miller.

As soon as Ms. Butterfield issued her standard greeting, Jane said, "Yes. Hello. I'd like to make another appointment with Mr. Hagger. Devin. Mr. Devin Hagger."

"He won't see you, Miss Ladling," Ms. Butterfield replied, as professional as could be. "In fact, I'm supposed to inform you that you are not to contact him again. Ever."

"But I have questions," she said with a pout. "Questions he should want to answer, by the way. If he didn't kill Tony Miller, I can help him clear his name. For free! Other people have offered me big bucks to do it." Kind of big bucks. In the same way a dollar was bigger than a dime. Whatever!

"He's not interested. If you enter the premises, I'm under strict orders to alert security. Be assured, I always obey orders." There was a crackling pause. Then a whispered, "But he'll be leaving the building at a quarter to eleven for a lunchtime appointment. If you're in the parking lot..."

"Oh, thank you, Ms. Butterfield! I owe you a dozen more cupcakes."

"I know. See that you pay up."

Jane was grinning as they disconnected. One kind deed had reaped a priceless reward! Talk about delicious fruit!

Hoping to hunt down Beau, she refocused on her laptop and opened the video feed streaming from the cameras positioned around the Garden. She planned to ask if they could trade vehicles for the day. Just in case Hagger had a standing order to prevent hearses from entering his parking lot. Except it wasn't Beau on patrol, but Holden.

The handsome vet was in the process of stalking a visitor. Who happened to be a ninety-four-year-old widower who'd come by the Garden every October for the past thirteen years to speak with his deceased wife. She lived in plot 238.

Not exactly a danger to the cemetery or Jane herself, but Holden definitely got an A for effort. The guys at Peach State Security took their job seriously.

There'd been no vehicle swap. One, she didn't know Holden well enough to trade cars. And two, she'd already worked up another plan. Park across the street and walk to Mr. Hagger's building. And that's exactly what she did.

Wind blustered, and the sky darkened with a coming storm. Still, she waited at the curb next to the lawyer's sleek black Mercedes. The second she detected his thumping footsteps, she popped up and blocked his path to the driver-side door.

Eyes narrowing, he came to an abrupt halt. "I have nothing to say to you, Miss Ladling."

With a leather briefcase in hand—a possible club—he appeared more intimidating than before. Not that she was intimidated by him or anyone. She was dating Conrad Ryan, for goodness' sake, despite the certainty of the Ladling curse. Had anyone ever done anything braver?

"Answer a single question for me," she said, "and I'll go. You'll never, ever have to see me again…until the next time you see me." A scowl contorted his features, and she hurried on. "Why did you visit Reggie Belfry at the hospital the day of his injury?"

Hagger ran his tongue over his teeth. "That's privileged information."

"That's not an answer." Or was it? "Was he already your client? Or perhaps he *is* your client even now?" *Mental note: Ask Conrad.* "Maybe he's your partner in crime. Did you pay him to murder Tony?"

"And that's a second, third and fourth question." With menace in every step, Hagger strode forward once again, closing in on her. Where had the unfazed barrister gone? "Your snooping is gonna get you into trouble. You keep at it, and you may not like what you find. Or who finds you."

"Is that a threat?"

"It's a truth."

When Jane remained in place, refusing to flee, he ran his tongue over his teeth. Okay then. Point made. She offered him a sunny smile. "You have a temper, Mr. Hagger. The murderer did too, considering he beat Tony with a bag of rocks. I guess we'll be seeing each other again, after all." With a little finger wave, she turned, and all but skipped toward her hearse.

"Come near me again," he called, "and I'll file a restraining order against you."

"That only makes you seem guiltier," she called back, without glancing over her shoulder.

Rather than drive home, she opted to take a stroll through town and clear her head before the storm broke. Maybe she'd spy Beau again, since he'd sent Holden to the Garden in his place. This time, she'd do better about remaining in the shadows. Except, it wasn't Beau she found, but Tiffany Hotchkins and Abigail Waynes-Kirkland. The duo exited Pay Dirt Pawn, laughing.

The wealthy widow and elegant brunette spotted Jane, glowered, and moved into her path. Okay, so, maybe she might be reaping *this* awful reward for ambushing Hagger.

"Hello, ladies," she offered politely. "Dig up any graves lately?"

A flush darkened Abigail's cheeks. "How are Fiona and Beau? Arrested for murder yet?"

Tiffany smirked at Jane. "Rumor is, *you're* the one who did the deed. All to make some extra cash."

Oh! That danged Ashley Katz! *She's for sure my next stop.* "I have another theory. You claim you were on vacation the night of my party, yes?" Jane whipped out *Truth Be Told* and a pen. "What if you two secretly remained in town to kill Tony, knowing I'd be desperate to exonerate my accused friends? An act of cold-blooded revenge." On that note, these ladies could have hired Ashley Katz to cast blame on Jane. In fact, that might be the reason they'd visited a pawn shop—they needed more money to meet the reporter's increasing demands. "Where did you say you went? Do you happen to have receipts?"

In unison, the pair paled. They shared a panicked look. Abigail muttered, "We didn't do it!"

"You're not pinning this on us," Tiffany barked.

They bolted, skirting around her. Well. That was suspicious. Up the suspect list they went.

Jane composed a mental note to speak with the pair soon, after she'd dealt with Ms. Katz and smoothed out her theories involving Belfry and Hagger.

All right. Enough meandering about town. The head clearing had failed. She made her way back to the hearse, mind whirling. *Had* Belfry and Hagger worked together to take out Tony? Because this scenario had lots more pizazz than Belfry taking care of matters on his own. And what of Emma? What if the *three* of them had worked together?

Maybe Emma and Hagger were partners, and Belfry the patsy. Hagger might intend to sink Belfry's defense the way he'd (allegedly) tried to sink Fiona's.

Thunder cracked as Jane climbed inside her vehicle. She started the engine but didn't drive off yet. Rather, she typed a text to Emma: *I know we aren't working together anymore, but I'm hoping you'd like to learn the truth about Tony's death...which might have come about differently than you think. Help me help you by telling me about Reggie Belfry's physical altercation with Tony.*

As she waited for Emma's response, Jane texted Fiona to ask about the sheriff. Then she sent a group message to Team

Truth, inviting everyone over for dinner to meet Rolex's new girlfriend. Everyone but Conrad. She decided to phone him on the drive to the Headliner offices. She just, well, she missed his voice. Which meant nothing. Only that he had a pleasant timbre.

Still no response from Emma. But everyone else replied right away, accepting the invite. Fiona also responded privately.

Fionality: *He's better all the time! In fact, he's gonna meet Thomas and his family this weekend.*

Thomas, her son. The relationship between Fiona and Sheriff Moore must be progressing to the next level. How wonderful.

After a chat with Ashley Katz, Jane would go to the grocery store. She prepared a quick menu in her head. Fried green tomatoes and okra, bacon wrapped jalapeño poppers with extra cream cheese, meatloaf sandwiches, oh and dessert. Banana pudding with the name brand wafers and lots of homemade whipped cream. Maybe a pie or two. Or a cake. Or both.

After buckling up, she turned on a little heat, activated the fancy, hands free thingy Beau had installed in the dash and dialed Conrad.

"Hello, Jane." His husky tone sent shivers down her spine. The perfect accompaniment to the warm air spilling from the vents. "What can I do for you?"

See! Pleasant timbre! "You can agree to come to dinner tonight," she said, easing the hearse onto the road. The sky finally opened up and showered raindrops over her windshield. With a flick of her finger, she engaged the wipers. "I'm having Team Truth over to meet Cartier. A cat."

Wait. She blinked, then squinted. Wow. When had the world gotten so blurry? Probably time to swap out the wipers.

"You're cooking? I will absolutely be there," he replied. "Wyatt might be with me. But when did you get a second cat?"

"I didn't. I'm cat-sitting. It's a long story. I'll explain later. And please do bring Wyatt." His foster brother. She'd met the charmer only once, but he'd left a huge impression. "Any news you can share on our case?" she asked, fighting a sudden yawn. Oh wow. Fatigue washed over her. She might have to take a quick catnap after leaving the grocery store.

"*Our* case?" His decadent chuckle crackled over the line. Unfortunately, his amusement didn't last long. "We released Mr. Belfry. He hasn't been ruled out, but we don't have a smoking gun yet." The more he spoke, the more his voice struck her as far off and tinny. "Something his attorney happily pointed out."

Thump. Thump. Thump. Her heart began to pound in her chest, signaling panic. Thing was, she wasn't the least bit panicked. Was she? "Is his attorney named Devin Hagger?"

"He might be."

Practically a confirmation. Important. In need of pondering. But focusing made her head hurt. Bad. "Conrad, I…I'm not feeling so hot right now. Maybe I should reschedule."

"You do sound off." Concern seeped from his voice. "What's wrong, sweetheart?"

"I don't know." Approaching a red light, she knew she was supposed to press the brake, but moving her foot became an impossible task. Unless she was supposed to do something else? Her mind couldn't process…thoughts fragmented…*think!* Why couldn't she think?

The car lurched forward, wipers swishing back and forth, clearing raindrops—revealing a truck coming from the left. She'd crossed lanes? She should do something. Yes? Muscles tensing, she yanked on the steering wheel—yes! She'd cleared the light without slamming into the other vehicle. Hadn't she? A horn blared as she struggled for air she couldn't catch. Sweat broke out across her brow and along the back of her neck.

"What's going on, Jane?" Conrad's concern grew, giving her name a hard punch. In the background, papers rustled. "Pull over. Now."

"Bad idea. Can't see real well." Her vision fuzzed again, and this time the world constricted. "Just gonna stop." But though she fought to lift her foot from the gas and press the brake, her limb still refused to obey. She even lost her hold on the steering wheel as her body went boneless.

Up ahead, blobs of silver, blue and white passed through another intersection, coming from both the left and right sides. Was this...the end? Her heart pounded harder.

"Jane? Tell me you've stopped."

"Promise you'll care for Rolex." More horns blared as she barreled straight ahead. "Conrad, I may be falling for y—" A high-pitched ring erupted in her ears, the world around her blackening.

Impact! Metal crunched and gears ground as her brain rattled against her skull. Her body flung forward and ricocheted back. The darkness consumed her.

CHAPTER ELEVEN

"Rules are the foundation of any game. Without a foundation, you will fall."
Holden Bishop, security expert

"Jane!"

The door to Jane's hospital room swung open, and Conrad rushed in. Distress etched every line of his ashen face, and her chest clenched. On the ambulance ride over, the paramedics had stuffed an oxygen cannula into her nose. As the fuzziness in her mind had faded, she'd remembered what she'd almost said to the special agent as she'd lost control of her body and the car.

Clearly, they needed to break up. Today.

"To my immense shock, I'm okay," she told him as he clutched her hand in his. "Just a bump on the head and a little whiplash." And oh wow, he'd gotten here in record time, beating even Fiona and Beau, who she'd only had a chance to phone ten minutes ago.

The paramedics had tended to her gash before driving her to Pinetum Regional for X-rays. Which she'd received right here in her room. A tech had wheeled in a giant machine with a long robotic arm. She just hadn't seen a doctor yet…but that might be because she had refused to see anyone but Dr. Price. Why not make the best of the situation?

"But, um, Conrad." She looked anywhere but him. "We really need to talk."

"Not necessary. I can tell you how the conversation goes. You'll suggest we break up. I'll refuse. You'll be secretly relieved, and we'll both act as if the topic was never broached. Let's just save time and skip ahead to the never broached portion of the afternoon." He heaved a shuddering breath. "If you ever crash your car again…" His eyes closed for a moment. "Don't get into another accident, Jane. I'm not sure I can survive this kind of stress a second time."

"Don't blame me. Blame my body. She betrayed me for no good reason. But, um, about that breakup." Her stomach churned. "I really think we should, you know, do it. Maybe see other people. Well, I should. You shouldn't. You should mourn my loss for months to come. Perhaps years."

He kissed her knuckles. And ignored her babbling. "Have you had any symptoms of sickness before today?"

"Nope. Not even the tiniest ache. But about our relationship being fractured beyond repair. We—"

The door swung open again, and a very handsome black man in scrubs strode inside. "I hear you requested me, Miss Ladling. You were in a car accident, I see." He glanced up from the chart he held then did a double take when he spotted Conrad. "Special Agent Ryan. Hello."

Conrad nodded a greeting. It was clear he had no intention of leaving her side for any reason. A very sweet gesture. Precious even. A memory she would forever cherish. But he might object to her questioning of the doctor. Or he might cheer her on. No reason to risk it.

"Um, Conrad. Since we're in the middle of a breakup—"

"Already back together," he told her, stubborn to his core.

"—I'd like some time alone with Dr. Price. To discuss my private medical condition."

Conrad pursed his lips, but he also nodded. "Take care of her," he said, his firm tone conveying a clear message: *or else*. He kissed Jane's brow, the tip of her nose, then her mouth, careful to avoid the bandaged area.

Her heart was racing as he strode from the room.

"I recognize you." Dr. Price set the chart aside and approached the gurney. "You run the cemetery. And you're dating the agent."

"We're only kind of dating. Maybe?" The muscles in her neck trembled with weakness as she shifted. "Trust me. It surprised me, too."

"He's an…interesting guy."

"Very much so." As the doctor began his examination, she said, "Listen. I'm working the Miller case. Hunting the killer." Why not be blunt and save time? "I know you had rounds in this hospital the day someone stole those opioids. Which also happens to be the same day Reggie Belfry came in with injuries from a fight with the victim. What I don't know is whether or not Emma Miller visited him or if you overheard Belfry's conversation with his attorney."

Dr. Price paused, blinking at her with his dark eyes fringed with thick lashes. Lucy was right. He really was a dreamboat. Wait! Jane's mind wasn't yet operating at full capacity, so it took her thoughts a minute to catch up with little details detected by her gaze. Had he stiffened when she'd mentioned Emma Miller?

Did he know the nurse who worked for a rival doctor? Had the two bumped into each other occasionally? Did Emma crush on him? Because wowzer. He just got hotter the longer you looked at him.

"I'm not allowed to talk about patients with anyone other than law enforcement," he said.

"I'm almost a private investigator. Does that count?"

"No." He flashed a pin light in front of her face, all business.

Hoping to gauge his reactions, Jane tried another route–conversational diarrhea. It had worked in the past. "Isn't it interesting how Emma was, or maybe *is*, dating Reggie Belfry? We can talk about that, since it's not medical. Who would ever pair such an odd couple? But love is powerful, amiright?"

His face scrunched up like he tasted something sour. "They are definitely not dating. She went out with him a few times, but nothing came of it. She was too busy dealing with Tony's harassment."

Uh, he seemed to know a lot about the nurse. Jane fidgeted with the corner of her blanket. Something was here. Could Dr. Price be the murderer's accomplice? Mighty convenient that he'd sent a timestamped video message to his staff the night of the murder. From a mystery party, no less.

"How much time have you spent with Ms. Miller?" she asked.

He scowled at Jane. "I don't think I like what you're implying."

"What *am* I implying?" she asked, feigning innocence.

His scowl only deepened. "Tony showed up here at the hospital a few times while Emma–Nurse Miller–did rounds with Dr. Garcia. Tony demanded to know who she was dating, then threatened to put the guy in the hospital and ruin any happiness she found."

Well, well, well. The lawyer must have been eaten up with jealousy. "Did Belfry fight back, sending Tony to the emergency room as well?"

"I'm not saying he did. But I'm not saying he didn't, either."

Meaning yes. He did. So, even Tony had visited the hospital the day the opioids were stolen.

Had he swiped the drugs? If his prints were the only ones found on the syringe… Were they? He *had* wanted to kill someone, judging by the search history on his burner phone. Well, one of his burner phones. Wait. He'd planned to stab his victim, not drug them. He'd even carried a knife in his pocket.

A knife he hadn't used. Hmm. Had he been too out of it after being whacked with rocks? Or was there another reason?

Dr. Price schooled his features, as if realizing he'd let too much slip. "Any lingering headache?"

"No, the pain has faded," she assured him. Was it strange that Emma had shared so many details about her no-strings dating life with Dr. Price? Especially considering Tony's vow. Or maybe she'd been so upset and fatigued by her husband's behavior, she'd needed to share with someone, and she'd chosen her co-workers. "Is there anything you remember about the night of Mr. Miller's murder that could help me prove you—" and Fiona and Beau— "are innocent of the crime?"

His eyebrows drew together, reluctance stamped all over his handsome face. "I heard Tony argue with a short, balding man, who claimed he wouldn't pay off anyone else. That, if Tony attacked another of Emma's dates, he'd go to jail."

Well. Rather than solicit work, Hagger might have paid Belfry not to press charged against Tony for engaging in fisticuffs. Had Belfry then demanded more money, making Hagger feel he had no other choice but murder?

Dang, she excelled at this.

The doctor finished his exam, asked her a few questions,

and made notes in her chart. "The X-rays show nothing is broken. But I'm prescribing a painkiller and a muscle relaxer for whiplash. By morning, that weakness in your neck and shoulders is going to translate into pain."

"Any idea about why I blacked out and lost control of my body?"

"Not yet. We're still waiting for the results of your blood tests. I should know something soon. If all looks good, we'll get you discharged."

Fair enough. "Thank you," she said. "For everything."

He nodded and moved toward the door, but paused when she called, "Hey, are you single, Dr. Price? I'm asking for a friend. Well, a possible friend. I'm not all in yet. But I notice you aren't wearing a wedding ring."

The muscles in his shoulders bunched. "I am very much *not* single." He left then.

Ohhhh. Sore topic? Maybe. But who was the dreamboat dating?

Conrad re-entered the room with Beau and Fiona on his heels.

"Oh, hon." Fiona elbowed the boys aside to reach her first. "Tell me you're okay. I mean it, tell me right this second. I've got to hear the words come out of your mouth." She patted Jane's cheeks and fluffed her pillows.

"I'm okay. Honest. I'm going to be discharged as soon as my blood tests come in."

"I'll stay over tonight, my sweet baby girl, and I'll see to your every need." Fiona took her other hand. "I'll make you all the blueberry pancakes you can hold."

"*I'll* be staying with her tonight." A stern-faced Conrad returned to her side. "I'll sleep on the couch, but I *will* be there."

"But…blueberry pancakes," she said, nearly whimpering. A never ending supply. Because that was how many she could hold. So close to Heaven on Earth! Wait, what if they both stayed the night? Then she could have the best of both worlds. Except, what about Sheriff Moore? He needed Fiona more than Jane did.

"Sorry, sweetheart, but this is non-negotiable. Beau?" Conrad nodded at her friend. "Tell her."

"I directed Isaac to the Tow Yard to look at the hearse. He sent me a text," Beau said, tapping a button on the screen of his phone, then read, "Someone tampered with the exhaust system of Jane's car, causing a leak of carbon monoxide into the cabin. At first glance, and considering the age of the hearse, the damage can pass as normal wear and tear. But the hole is too clean. Whoever did it is good, but I'm better."

What! Someone had purposely harmed her? Carbon monoxide explained the fuzziness and the headache and why things had snapped crystal clear once she'd breathed in sweet, sweet oxygen in the ambulance.

But why? Who? "Isaac must be wrong. We would've caught anyone messing with the hearse on the Garden's security footage." Unless... *Lucy* had done it before banging on her door. But no. The loan officer wouldn't. Would she?

No. No, she wouldn't.

"The culprit could have worked while you were parked in town," Conrad said.

Good point. She huffed, already rolling through other possible suspects. Everyone she'd seen strolling along the sidewalks. Any shopkeeper unhappy with her questioning. Robby, of course. Tiffany and Abigail, too.

Jane sucked in a breath. If anyone wanted her harmed, it was Robby, Tiffany and Abigail.

See! Not Lucy.

"I'm staying with you," Conrad reiterated. "I'll also be speaking with people in town."

"Fine. I'll pick you over pancakes, but only this once."

And she refused to ponder the immense amount of relief she experienced at the thought of being near him a while longer. Trembling now, she offered her hand to him, and her special agent linked their fingers. "But you owe me so big."

The corners of his mouth twitched. "Don't worry, sweetheart. I always pay my debts."

JANE WAS HOME, in pajamas, and stretched out comfortably on the couch by 5:00 p.m. with a full house by 6:30. Beau, Fiona, Trick, Isaac and Holden migrated to and from the kitchen, where Fiona made her world-famous pancakes. *Getting both, after all!* Sheriff Moore had launched an investigation from home. Meaning, he'd sent his deputies to town to question folks while he attended the Q and A via a smart phone.

Rolex and Cartier perched on the mantel above the hearth, both hissing at anyone who neared. They were just so stinking cute together.

Conrad sat on the coffee table, unwilling to leave Jane's side or let go of her hand. He also quizzed her about her activities the past week, kissing her knuckles each time she answered. She tried so hard not to love it. But then he did it again.

To the right, glass shattered. Jane jolted, then winced. Dr. Price had been wrong about being sore tomorrow. The pain had already arrived. Staying as still as possible, she slid her gaze over the living room—a vase lay in pieces beneath the mantel. Beneath Rolex, to be more specific.

Surely he hadn't pushed it off. The little angel was, well, an angel.

"I'll clean up the mess," Beau said, already heading for the pantry, where the broom and dustpan were stored.

Conrad used his free hand to type a text to someone. It was then that she remembered his plan to bring Wyatt to tonight's dinner.

"Your brother," she said with a groan. "Did I ruin your time with him?"

"No worries." He brought her hand to his face and rubbed her knuckles against his stubbled jawline. "We've already rescheduled."

Another mantelpiece knickknack hit the floor, and this time, Jane saw it happen. Yep, Rolex, her angel, was responsible.

"I think my baby is upset about our relationship." She chewed on her bottom lip, her earlier fears rushing back. "What if this is a sign we should break up?"

"It isn't a sign, Jane. I'm not going anywhere." He released her at last, but only to drop two pills in her palm. Her prescriptions. Next, he passed her a glass of sweet tea. "Be a good patient. Take your meds."

"Sir, yes, sir," she said, because what else *could* she say? Down the hatch.

A knock hammered at the door, and excitement sparked. Must be Lucy.

"I'll get it," Trick said.

"No! Let Holden get it," she rushed out, sitting up. Ow, ow, ow!

Frowning, Conrad cupped her nape and eased her onto her mound of pillows. "If I have to lay beside you and hold you down to keep you from trying to do too much, I will."

"What kind of threat is that?" she muttered, wanting to smile. Bossy Conrad was so cute.

Another knickknack hit the floor.

"Why do I have to be the one to open the door?" Holden

asked, even as he strode over and turned the knob. And there was Lucy, adorable in a red T-shirt and jeans. "Ah. Okay. I get it now."

"Oh. You," Lucy said, flustered as she edged around him, entering the foyer.

"Yes," he replied, moving with her, ensuring they remained face to face. He was grinning like a big, bad wolf. "Me."

So. She clearly remembered Holden.

"If—if you'll excuse me." The loan officer darted around him, scanning the area. "Jane!" A gasp parted her lips, and she rushed over, radiating genuine concern. "What happened? Are you all right?"

Conrad stood, offering his seat to the loan officer. "I won't be far," he said as Lucy sank onto the coffee table and dropped her purse at her feet.

Jane explained the situation, leaving out the part about the tampered exhaust system. No reason to worry her… friend. Yes, the term just felt right. After almost dying, things were clearer than ever.

Deciding to be forthright, she asked the loan officer *the* question. "Why didn't you tell me you and Holden smacked into each other at the party?"

Cheeks flushing, Lucy leaned forward and whispered, "I've been trying to forget that part of the night. I didn't want to relive it. Seriously, Jane, it was one of the most humiliating moments of my life."

"How so?" She had to know. For the case.

"He didn't tell you?" Lucy's eyes went wide, and her volume dipped even lower. "I mean, you're friends with him. Or so I assume, since he's here and everything."

"We are friends, yes. But you didn't answer my question."

The other woman's flush deepened. "When I heard the scream, I thought someone had won the contest, so I headed back to my booth to pack up. I didn't get very far before Muscles plowed into me. I fell. He paused long enough to help me up and ask if I was okay. I...well, I kind of...kissed him. After Tony brought up Oliver, I'd started feeling sorry for myself, I guess, thinking I'd never find the right guy. But Muscles wrenched free and started running away from me, as if I repulsed him."

Ohhh. Okay, yes. Jane might not want to share that sort of story with others, either.

Lucy's nose wrinkled. "Wait. Did you think *I* might have killed Tony?"

Jane refused to lie. "I did. But only off and on, I promise! And now I'm certain you're innocent."

"I—I see," Lucy said, her chin trembling. "So you only pretended to be my friend to get information out of me?" She winced and stood. "Wow. More humiliation here at the Garden. Exactly what I didn't want tonight. If you don't mind, I'm gonna go."

"Please don't. Stay," she rushed out, guilt churning in her stomach. She'd made her new friend feel terrible, and oh, what an awful seed to plant. "It was nothing personal, I promise. I suspect everyone of murder."

"Jane, everything is personal, whether you want it to be or not." Lucy crossed her arms against her middle, vulnerable and wounded. "Have you ever suspected anyone else in this room of such a horrid crime?"

Jane licked suddenly dry lips. "Well. No. But—"

"Yeah, I'm definitely going." A humorless laugh filled the space between them. "I'm taking Cartier with me."

"Lucy." Jane attempted to rise, only to fall back against the pillows with a pained moan. Stupid pills. Why hadn't they kicked in yet? "I'm sorry," she called. But Lucy was already in possession of her pet, striding out the door.

As Holden tore off after her, remorse and sadness warred

within Jane, and both sucked. She recognized a good thing when it severed her from its life. Rolex recognized it, too, and released a plaintive, pitiful meow.

"Jane, you can't be friends with Lucy," Trick announced.

Isaac nodded with enthusiasm. "There's a hundred percent chance she's the murderer. I'd put money on it."

What? "No!"

"Holden only goes for bad girls," Beau explained with a shrug.

"Well, so does Conrad. Obviously. His girlfriend has gone to jail," Jane said, and snickers erupted all around, as if she'd made some sort of joke. "Besides, there's a first time for everything. Lucy is wonderful." *And I lost her. Destroyed the friendship before it even had a chance to fully bloom.*

Maybe it was the high-octane emotions of the day, but Jane did something odd. She burst into tears.

"All right," Conrad thundered at her audience. "Everyone out."

Jane only cried harder. "I don't know why I'm doing this." She pressed the heel of her hands to her eyes. "It's embarrassing."

Fiona rushed to her side to pat her cheek. "It most certainly is not embarrassing, hon. Those tears are little drops of love seeping from cracks in your heart. But there's no reason for them today. You'll win her back. You can do anything. Now, I'm gonna go, so Conrad can comfort you properly. I left a big stack of blueberry pancakes in the kitchen, but you aren't allowed to eat them until you've laughed at least twice. Understand?"

"Yes, ma'am," she said, more forlorn than ever.

"Good girl." Footsteps. Hinges squeaking. The soft snick of the door closing for good. Then Conrad and Jane were alone. He did as threatened and carefully maneuvered onto the couch, taking her in his arms and helping her burrow into his warmth. Beneath her ear, his heart raced.

He kissed the top of her head. "Everything will be okay, sweetheart."

Through her sniffling, she asked, "How can you know that?"

"Just like Fiona said. You are Jane Ladling, and you can do anything. Even tame a rare and wild officer inspector detective special agent."

Well, he wasn't wrong. Her sniffles turned to giggles as a warm wave of euphoria swept over her. "Do you want to know what will make me feel better than assurances?" Did her words sound slightly slurred? Uh-oh. The pain meds must have kicked in at last. Oh well. Onward and upward. "If you take your shirt off. Skin-to-skin contact is very therapeutic. I've heard muscles make everything better."

He burst out laughing—but he also took off his shirt, revealing pecs for days and an eight-pack glazed in bronze.

Goodness gracious! He was magnificent. "And you're all mine," she muttered, snuggling closer. Mmm. His heat. The softness of his skin…like velvet poured over smooth rocks.

"Finally I get to witness medicated Jane in person rather than over the phone." Amusement tinged his voice. "Just so you know, you can say anything tonight. I won't be taking advantage of you, but I will be loving and hating every moment of this delightful torture."

She adored the way his love drum pounded beneath her cheek. And if "love drum" wasn't a thing, it should be. "If it wasn't for the Ladling curse, I might have married you and had a dozen babies by now."

He swallowed. "Oh yeah? Tell me more."

"Should we get a couple's cackets?" she asked him instead, then frowned. "Casekets. Casss-kets." Better.

"How about we live together before we plan to die together?"

"I could never leave my cemetery. The residents would revolt." Wait. She gently traced a pucker of raised tissue with the tip of her nail. A scar. Small and round, just above his heart.

"Got shot in the line of duty." He offered the tidbit about his past without flinching while sifting strands of her hair through his fingers. "A suspect didn't want to go in for questioning."

"Well, that sucks. I hate that you were in pain because someone was dumb enough to protest a free tour of GBH headquarters. Something *I've* never gotten, thank you very much. But I can't say I regret the scar. Me-ow," she said, pretending to scratch him.

He snickered, clasped her fingers and kissed her knuckles. "Like scars, do you?"

"Apparently." She thought she might like everything about this man. The very reason she was keeping him.

Uh...keeping him?

No. Nope. Not happening. Probably.

CHAPTER TWELVE

"Do your victory dance when it seems like you're losing. It confuses competitors."
Fiona Lawrence, retired schoolteacher

Three days later, Jane pushed a protesting Conrad out the door and into the fading sunlight. "Go on. Get out of here. The office is desperate for your full time return! If they're going to solve any cases, they need to borrow your brain more than I need pampering or protection. Okay. Bye."

She tried to shut the door, but he stuck his foot out, stopping her. "I will be back tomorrow morning," he said, stern.

"No!" Trying to hide her growing panic, she faked a laugh. "Come back in a week. Or two. Probably should make it three to be safe."

"Tomorrow." He removed his foot and stalked to his car.

"Fine! Tomorrow," she bellowed, finally shutting the door. Dang, dang, dang. What was she going to do?

Jane paced through her living room. Since the accident, the awful man had cooked her breakfast each morning while waiting for someone from Peach State Security to show up and act as her guard. Then he'd left for work for a few hours, only to return with dinner. He'd spend the night in Jane's guest room. Now she felt ready to live again—without him!

He tempted her beyond reason. Made her want things she shouldn't. So, he for sure had to go.

Gah! But she missed him already. Thankfully, there was a cure for that—investigation. There'd been no leads on the case of the sabotaged hearse, but *she* placed all blame on Tony's killer. She must be getting close to the truth.

Of course, there'd been no new leads in Tony's case, either. Probably because she'd been out of commission and all. Really, how did GBH solve a crime without her and her deductions? Worse, she'd received no word from Lucy, despite leaving a lengthy voice mail apology. And also texted apologies. And also many other voicemail apologies. And the letter Jane had Conrad mail.

But she wasn't going to think about her massive failure in the friendship department. Or the fact that her cat had stopped speaking to her. Or the pure joy of having Conrad so close, so often. Nope. Today, she focused solely on Tony's case.

Jane texted Ms. Katz. *Are you ready to meet in person?*

Put her life on hold just because someone might be gunning for her? No. Jane would get out there and do what she did best: cause so much trouble the killer eventually revealed themself to escape the torment. Or something like that.

Though she waited several minutes, she received no response. Decided to ignore her like Emma Miller? No problem. On to phase two of her agenda. Jane phoned Fiona.

"You want to interview a suspect tonight?" she asked the second her friend answered. "Reggie Belfry is hosting some kind of dinner party in the city." Having spent a lot of hours stuck in bed, going over the photos and notes she'd taken, logging the chef's upcoming events, she knew there was no better time to get a face-to-face with him.

Was he the lynch pin of suspects?

"A girl's night?" Fiona chortled. "A thousand percent I do. Pick me up at six."

"See you then." Jane spent the day catching up on chores around the Garden as well as the cottage, trying to re-win Rolex's affections and fortify her defenses against Conrad.

Without meds, "screw the curse" didn't seem like such a brilliant idea.

Or was it?

Argh! By 5:45, she was cleaned up and sitting behind the wheel of her rental. A white, four-door sedan with all the bells and whistles but no personality. Conrad had taken the hearse to do the repairs himself. During the last case, she'd learned he liked to rebuild old cars.

By 5:58, her friend was climbing in the passenger seat. "I'm so glad we're doing this, hon." Fiona patted her hand. "I've missed you."

"I've missed you, too." Several blocks later, she reached the highway exit. "What did you tell the sheriff about our activities? The whole truth?"

"Are you kidding? Tell a sworn officer of the law that the chef preparing our dinner is a suspected murderer just when GBH is sniffing around me once again? No. I stopped at a special girl's night."

"Ah, smart." As soft as Jane had been feeling toward Conrad lately, she'd opted to go with total silence. Seriously. She'd often peered over at him for no good reason. Leaned her head upon his strong shoulder. Curled up against him just because. Yeah, silence was best. He didn't need to know what she was up to tonight; he might start protesting her involvement like before and harken back to the car accident.

Wait. "GBH suspects you again?" Jane screeched.

Fiona flinched. "I think they might. Hightower called my attorney earlier today to schedule another interview."

Jane's grip tightened on the steering wheel. "I am figuring this out, I promise you."

"I know you are. That's why there's no reason for me to worry. Now, I've been thinking about your Lucy problem," Fiona said, changing the subject. "If you want to win her back, you've got to do a grand gesture."

Jane allowed the switch because her friend was right; she had this. Nothing to worry about. "That's a marvelous idea. But what kind of—oh! I know." The answer crystalized in an instant, and she wondered why she hadn't thought of it before. "Lucy's entire world revolves around her cat." As it should. "Oliver, her ex, recently attempted to abduct the little beauty. If Beau and I pay this Oliver guy a visit, we can ensure Cartier is forever safe. Lucy will have no choice but to like me again."

Except one nagging thought plagued her. If Beau and his buddies were right, and Lucy were a quote unquote bad girl, then she might have created the imaginary Oliver as an excuse to meet with Tony, because she'd planned to kill him all along. And what better reason to meet with Jane and get close to her car?

Gah! No. Wrong. She wasn't heading down that road again. For once, she was going to think the best of someone.

"The perfect gesture," Fiona said. "In fact, we can visit Beau when we finish with the chef. Better not to put things off, I always say."

"Agreed." They could also ask him if GBH had set up another interview with him and find out if he had uncovered any leads of his own. He'd been so quiet lately, preoccupied with his own mystery.

Determination spilled through Jane as she parked the

rental at their destination. Hmm. The lot was surprisingly full tonight.

She and Fiona emerged and braved the chilly October night.

"Did you make a reservation?" her friend asked.

"I did." Under a fake name. "But only because I didn't want Belfry to pack up and go home when no one else showed up. I never expected this." Strobe lights pulsed from the side of a graffiti laden brick wall, illuminating a crowd lined up around the building.

Jane and Fiona bypassed the throng to reach a man with a clipboard who stood at the door. Above him hung a sign that read "Feast of Horrors. Welcome to Le Sang."

Well. Belfry had rebranded.

"We have a reservation under the name Agatha Drew," Jane said.

He checked the clipboard, then nodded and waved two fingers at someone. She frowned as a woman dressed in a sexy cop costume came forward and held out a pair of plastic handcuffs.

"You have the right to eat whatever Chef Reggie prepares you," the newcomer said with a monotone voice, reaching for Jane's hands. "There are no menus, so anything else you wish to order will be denied to you. You have a right to leave if you disagree. If you don't want to leave, you'll sit down and enjoy yourself."

She almost wrenched back, but in the end, for the sake of the case, she allowed herself to be handcuffed and led forward by the "cop."

Fiona followed. "What is even going on right now?" she demanded at low volume.

"Chef Reggie was recently freed from prison after killing a guy. Allegedly," the woman added. "This is his celebration dinner. Enjoy. Or not."

So Belfry was using his connection to Tony's case to fuel his career? Talk about motive!

Most Wanted posters decorated the walls and concrete blocks separated the tables. The backs of the chairs reminded her of jail cell bars.

The hostess escorted Jane and Fiona to a small round table in the back, where she removed the cuffs. Too few wait staff manned the place, running to and from the kitchen, each dressed as either a guard or an inmate. One of the inmates plopped two glasses on the table, both filled with a frozen cocktail and smelling of coconut. Next came a plate with what looked to be deep dish pizza slices.

"Enjoy the Colada Confessions and Femme Fatale Flamiche," the guy said before bailing.

Fiona leaned across the table. "Flay-me-chee?"

"I thought we'd get a more personal experience," Jane muttered, scooping a slice onto her plate. "We've got to speak with Belfry."

"Go on back to the kitchen," Fiona suggested. "No one will notice. Actually, I doubt anyone will care. But just in case, I'll stay here and watch for security. If necessary, I'll stage a distraction."

"Perfect!" Was there any better friend than Fiona Lawrence? Jane kissed her cheek and popped to a stand. She darted across the restaurant. When a waitress shouldered past the swinging double-doors, carrying plates of...something slimy, Jane waited a beat, then shot inside the kitchen.

Stainless steel refrigerators, counters and prep stations greeted her, along with the smell of burning food. Reggie Belfry stood beside a man Jane didn't recognize. The stranger wore a dapper chef's hat as he sprinkled a pinch of spice over a pastry.

Belfry griped the other man's wrist and forced him to dump the spices over the dessert while shouting, "Am I the only one with a shred of talent, people? Do your job so I don't have to do it for you."

Jane smoothed the sides of her dress and approached Belfry. Would he recognize her from the party?

He shoved the newly spiced dish at Hat, barking, "Do it my way, the right way, or get out." Then he stalked to a six-burner gas range to stir whatever simmered in a large stockpot.

Hat noticed her approach, stepped in front of her to block, and snapped, "Guests aren't allowed in the kitchen."

"Oh, I'm not a guest. I'm an associate of the GBH." Not a lie. She skirted around him before he offered another protest. When she reached her target, she cleared her throat. "Hello, Mr. Belfry. I'd like to talk to you about the Tony Miller case." Excellent. Direct and to the point.

He flicked a narrowed glance in her direction. What he didn't do? Run away. "Yeah? So would hundreds of others."

No, he didn't recognize her. Honestly, she barely recognized him. He was taller than she'd expected and not nearly as wiry looking in person. His features had a more sculpted appearance.

"Yes, but the others can't shut down your restaurant if you refuse to answer." Okay, so, technically Jane couldn't either. But she still hadn't lied. Adopting her most confident posture—arms folded and chin up—she said, "Tell me about your relationship with Tony Miller."

Scowling, he turned to a counter, where a series of bowls and ingredients awaited him. He dumped different things inside them. "I'll tell you what I told the other agents. He was a lawyer. Do the math. Someone was bound to kill him. The end."

Jane etched notes into her mental files for Reggie Belfry—*Unpleasant person.* "What did you know about his ex-wife, Emma?"

A leering smile pulled at his thin lips. "I know she's a thirty-six C, always down for public PDA, and a cold fish in private. That's why I dumped her. A man has needs."

A shudder ran down Jane's spine. *Change "unpleasant person" to "revolting".*

Who was telling the truth, though? Belfry or Emma? He said he'd dumped her; she said they'd never gotten serious and had only gone on a few dates. Jane's guess? Reggie Belfry was trying to protect a fragile ego. He'd stalked the nurse at the cemetery, after all.

Had he killed Tony, hoping to blame Emma for the crime as payback? Had GBH gotten things right for once?

"Why did you sneak into the party at the Garden of Memories, after attempting to enter with a ticket?" Jane asked.

"Someone—Tony, I'm sure—mailed me the tickets a week apart. Crispy bacon and al dente. As if either one is an insult. And that's how he meant it, I'm sure," Belfry grumbled. "The guy at the door wouldn't let me in, since I didn't have an ID to match. I *had* to sneak it."

Wait. "How do you know Tony mailed you those tickets?"

"He texted me. After I blocked his number, he just went and got himself another."

That explained the second phone. Kind of. If the first number hadn't worked, why carry it around, along with a second phone and also his normal cell? Three cellular devices seemed excessive. "What did his messages say?"

"In the original, he invited me to the party and bragged about his plans to bang Emma. Said he wanted me to have a front-row seat. In the second, he pretended to be Emma and begged me for creepy cemetery sex." Belfry hiked up his shoulder while lowering his head, wiping a bead of sweat from his temple. "I admit, at the time, I'd hoped that one legit came from Em."

Jane's instincts pinged. As a lawyer, Tony knew to cover his tracks, hence the anonymity of pretending to be Emma. But why use a burner phone to make threats as yourself first?

What am I missing? "Do you still have those texts?"

With a harried expression, Belfry wiped his hands on a towel, swiped a cell from his chef's coat and keyed up a photo of the message supposedly from Tony, then turned the screen Jane's way. She snatched the device. With a swipe, she found a photo of the second message as well. Well. Exactly as advertised.

"Mind if I send myself a copy of these?" she asked, already punching in her number.

"Yes, I mind," he hissed, reaching for the phone.

Too late. Her phone dinged with the new messages. "Oops." Moving on. "I know you followed Emma at the party. Did you have her in your sights before the scream sounded? Or even when it occurred. What about afterward?"

He picked at a thread on his cuff. "Never heard the scream. By then, I'd already left."

Hmm. "Can you prove that?"

"Can you prove I hadn't?" More beads of sweat appeared on his forehead. "We're done here. If you've got other questions, call my lawyer."

"You mean Devin Hagger?"

"Not anymore." Belfry combined the contents of two bowls. Whatever he was making did not smell appetizing. "Hagger is the literal worst. Firing him was the best decision I've ever made."

Wait, wait, wait. "You fired him? Why?" Or was the firing as likely as Emma's dumping? Had Hagger dropped Belfry?

"The guy kept advising me to confess to the crime," the "chef" told her with a scowl. "Who does that?"

Someone who hoped to hide their own guilt, that was who. *Welcome back to the top of my list, Hagger.* "Why did you hire him in the first place, considering he covered up your fight with Tony?"

"He agreed to work for free. Why else?" Belfry passed a bowl of whatever that was to the sous chef and rooted through a pile of containers below the counter. "As you can see, I'm busy. So like I said, you can contact my lawyer if you—"

"Just one more question, then I'll go," she rushed out before he could finish the sentence. "Why did you fight Tony, where did this fight occur, and did Emma visit you in the hospital?" Technically, the three were stuck together, which meant, yes, Jane had expertly turned a triple into a single.

"The guy jumped me outside Em's house, so I taught him a lesson. And yeah, she visited me at the hospital. Long enough to call me a jerk and storm out, as if protecting myself was some sort of crime. But if that's the way Tony reacts just because a guy plays a little tonsil hockey with his ex, it's no wonder someone killed him. It was only a matter of time, if you ask me." Belfry turned his back on her then, letting her know he was done talking.

No problem. Jane had enough intel to keep her busy for days. Practically floating, she returned to the table—where she found Trick sitting with Fiona. He offered Jane an unapologetic smile.

"Why?" she demanded. How?

Trick shrugged his broad shoulders. "Conrad and Raymond know their women. They asked Peach State Security to play secret bodyguard."

And she hadn't sensed a thing. How irritating!

"I caught sight of him when he attempted to track you to the kitchen," Fiona told her.

Sigh. "Well, Trickster, I'll save you the trouble of guessing our next stop. We're headed to Beau's. If you warn him that we're coming, you can say goodbye to the cheesy chicken and rice casserole I just decided to bake for you."

"And you'll be grounded from my blueberry pancakes for three months, with no hope of obtaining a pardon," Fiona added with a nod.

He might have whimpered. "Ladies, consider my silence bought and paid for."

"Good boy." Fiona patted his cheek.

Trick escorted them to the rental, then disappeared somewhere in the darkness of the lot. As Jane drove along the highway, explaining everything she'd learned from Belfry, she knew Trick followed. And, yeah, okay, it was kind of nice having some muscle at her disposal, should a need arise.

"I bet Beau and his hacking skills can find out who sent Belfry those texts," Fiona said with a nod.

"They probably came from those burner phones Tony carried." But had Tony bought both...or had the killer stuffed one in his pocket? Tony could have planned to kill Belfry, while the murderer planned to kill Tony and blame Belfry.

Tomorrow night, Jane might stake out Emma's home. Or Hagger's. Or heck, Belfry's. Which one, which one? The lawyer desperate to assign blame, the widow with a connection to everyone involved, or the chef who couldn't tolerate any blows to his fragile ego?

Again Jane wondered if two or more had worked together. Was she missing something? Overlooking a key detail? Gah! Hadn't her gut told her this was a frame job? But who had framed whom? They all looked guilty!

As she parked under a lamp across the street from Peach State Security, Fiona gasped and proclaimed, "What in the world?"

Jane scanned—and gaped. Beau was striding along the lamp lit sidewalk, carrying a protesting woman over his shoulder, fireman-style. He disappeared inside the building a moment later.

Fiona's mouth opened and closed. "Should we…?"

"Go in and find out what's going on?" Jane finished for her, already unbuckling. "Yes. We absolutely should."

CHAPTER THIRTEEN

"Risk everything for the win. The alternative? Lose everything."
Beauregard Harden, security expert

Jane perched beside Fiona on Beau's couch. Beau and his new lady friend sat in chairs across from them. No one spoke, everyone waiting for someone else to steer the conversation. Jane was a little too busy gawking at the decor.

Things had certainly changed since the vet bought the building. Not the bank of floor to ceiling windows overlooking Prospect Street or the striking open concept loft with trendy and industrial architectural features. Those were the same. The difference came from the additions. A pair of black stilettos by the front door. A stunning beaded scarf tossed haphazardly over one of the kitchen chairs. Multi-colored bras dried on the coffee table. The new girl had been here a while.

With his pale hair sticking out in spikes and his eyes sharp, Beau appeared frazzled for the first time in their acquaintance. The woman, on the other hand, looked perfectly at ease. Delighted, even.

The newcomer wasn't an Aurelian Hills resident. She seemed to be the same age as Jane, and she was beyond beautiful, with long sable hair, flawless brown skin, and rich chestnut eyes.

Was she Beau's houseguest? Live-in girlfriend? Secret roommate?

Finally, the usually unflappable vet shattered the silence, saying, "Feeling better, Jane?"

"Much, thank you."

"Oh, for goodness' sake. Enough of this," Fiona burst out. "Someone tell us what's going on this instant or I'm going to throw a nightmare of a hissy fit."

Beau ran his tongue over his teeth. "Fiona, Jane, meet Sora Khatri, one of the worst people you'll ever have the displeasure of meeting. Sora, meet Fiona and Jane, two of the best."

"Hello." Not the least bit insulted, Sora gave them an adorable two finger wave. Then she smiled with sugary sweetness at Beau. "Do you plan to hold them captive, too?"

"No," he grated. "Just you."

Captive? What the *what*? Was this, like, a fun little game the two love birds played with each other? Because dang. The air fairly crackled with sexual tension.

"Would anyone like a glass of water?" Beau asked, using the same calm, measured tone. "Maybe tea? A juice?"

"What I'd like," Jane said, glancing between the pair, "is an explanation. Otherwise, I fear I'll be forced to launch a whole new investigation while Fiona is busy hissying."

He heaved a defeated sigh. "Miss Khatri witnessed something she shouldn't. Now, very bad men want her dead. She's remaining in my care–"

"Custody," the beauty interjected. "And please, ladies. Call me Sora."

"—whether she wants to or not," he continued without missing a beat. "Though I'm praying I'll be relieved of this duty sooner rather than later."

His custody? Was he still active in the military or something? Working for law enforcement?

"I don't want to remain with him, in case anyone is wondering." Sora batted long black lashes at Beau and smiled again, as if she'd merely commented on the weather. "But I would like that tea, honey pie. Please and thank you."

Honey pie? Hmm. Should Jane give Conrad a cute endearment? Something like *buttered buns*. Or hot pants. Tater tot? Sugar snap pea?

Wait. There would be no thinking about her special agent tonight. Especially when she'd begun to connect some dots. Beau had missed his cue at the murder mystery because he'd been guarding his guest. To keep Sora close, he must have stashed her somewhere on the property.

Did GBH know about her? He's said he'd explained some things to Conrad, but had he revealed the full truth or redacted certain details to keep Sora safe? "Well, now that this mystery is solved, I should probably get Fiona home to the Sheriff, so Trick can clock out for the night." She almost laughed when Beau double blinked. "Oh! Before we go, I need you to do me two favors."

He gave her a you-are-trying-my-patience look. "You know I'll do whatever you need, Janie. Anytime, anywhere."

Sora's lips pursed. "I believe I mentioned being thirsty for that tea."

Beau worked his jaw. "Be right back," he grated, standing. He stalked from the living room.

"We're only friends," Jane rushed to assure the other woman. "I have a boyfriend named Conrad. Well, I broke up with him, I think, but then he got back together with me. Mostly. There's a curse, you see. And—"

"Did I ask about your relationship with Beau?" Huffy, Sora leaped to her feet. "No, I did not. Because I don't care about him. He can see who he wants, when he wants. It makes no difference to me. Now, if you'll excuse me, please. I'm tired after working all day to bypass his security." That said, she marched from the living room, disappearing in the hallway, leading to the bedrooms.

Fiona reached over to pat Jane's hand. "Don't worry, hon. People who deny their feelings tend to react badly to the strangest things. Don't you think?"

Something about her tone suggested Jane should consider, perhaps, possibly applying those very wise words to her own life. Or not. Yeah, probably not.

Beau returned, a glass in hand, and glowered as soon as he noticed Sora's absence. With a huff of his own, he plopped into the chair he'd vacated and set the tea on a side table. "I told you," he muttered. "The worst."

"Yes. Well. About those favors you promised me. I need you to find out if anything can be learned from these texts to Reggie Belfry." Jane whipped out her phone and air dropped him the photos. "Also, can you track down a guy named Oliver…something? He is Lucy's ex-boyfriend, and he tried to steal Cartier. One day soon, you and I will pay him a visit and let him know such atrocious behavior won't be tolerated any longer."

"Don't worry about Oliver. Holden will take care of it. But I'll let you know about the numbers."

"How very sweet of Holden," Fiona remarked, wiggling her brows. No doubt her matchmaker's heart had skipped a beat, just like Jane's.

"I kind of need to go with him when he does it," she said.

"This is my grand gesture to win back Lucy's friendship. Make sure Holden knows that."

Beau let his head rest against his chair and peered up at the ceiling as if praying for patience. "Anything else?"

"Nope. That covers everything. Thanks, Bo-Bo." She and Fiona stood. "We can see ourselves out."

THE NEXT MORNING, after completing her chores around the cemetery, Jane drove straight to the Headliner offices. The first stop of many she planned for today. The time had come for her showdown with Ms. Ashley Katz.

Head high, she entered the lobby of Aurelian Hills Media, which housed the town's only AM station, an internet show called My Advice Is Yours, and the new and improved Headliner, both the app and paper division. There was even a space people could reserve to record a podcast.

The building was a hub of activity, but Jane didn't bother asking anyone for help. She strode down the hall as if she owned the place until she found the right door, then entered without bothering to knock.

A quick scan. Details hit her, one after the other. Small room. Big white board behind the desk. Curvy woman wearing a tailored white blouse, black calf length pencil skirt and blood red stilettos. The ends of her curly hair brushed the collar of her shirt. With her hands anchored on her hips, she faced the board. To the left, multiple monitors displayed the current happenings on the Headliner.

While unnoticed, Jane glanced over the board. A mess of names, photos and strings, with Tony's image at the top of it all. Emma's face had a big red X over it. So did Hagger's and Dr. Price's. There was a question mark over Dr. Garcia and

Reggie Belfry, as well as Jane, Fiona, Beau, Lucy and even Conrad.

"Why did you rule out Devin Hagger and Emma Miller?" Jane asked.

Ms. Katz whipped around, her dark eyes going wide. She pulled earbuds from her ears. "Jane Ladling." Frowning, she rushed to cover up the board using a sheet she'd attached to the top with large binder clips. "We meet at last."

"Why did you rule out Devin Hagger and Emma Miller?" Jane asked again.

After sitting behind the desk, Ms. Katz waved to the chairs in front of her. "Please, have a seat." Only after Jane smoothed the skirt of her dress and eased into the seat, as requested, did Ms. Katz continue. "Emma hired me to find her ex's murderer. Not something a killer would do. As for Hagger, a witness places him far from the crime scene at the time of Ms. Lawrence's scream."

So. Emma had double-dipped with her investigators, putting her fingers in every available cookie jar. More suspicious than ever! "Who is this supposed witness? Video footage might or might not disagree with their assessment." And their own placement.

"All right. I'll play this game." Ms. Katz fiddled with an extra binder clip on the desk. "I spoke with Lucy Chang last night. She spotted him about eight minutes before the scream while she was on a walk, then again upon her return. He isn't physically fit enough to make the necessary sprint between locations without showing signs."

A frown pulled at the corners of Jane's mouth. It was possible Lucy had seen Hagger on her way to the bridge in Eden Valley. But why hadn't she told Jane, the PI she'd originally hired?

Had it been anyone else, Jane would have etched their name in stone at the top of her suspect list. Yet, doubting

Lucy had caused nothing but problems. There *must* be a legitimate reason for her oversight.

"You believe Lucy's claim, though you still suspect her of murder?" Jane hadn't forgotten the question mark above her friend's photo. And Lucy *was* her friend, whether or not the other woman forgave her.

"Until I speak with Hagger again and confirm Chang's story, she remains a suspect. She is physically fit enough to make the sprint. And besides, she was closer to the murder, anyway."

Again, she'd said. Had Devin Hagger given Ms. Katz a full-on interview? "Or maybe you have a problem with anyone connected to me. Before we ever spoke, you wrote sneering remarks about my home."

"I wrote facts." Ashley picked up a pen and flipped open a notebook. "Speaking of, can you prove Fiona Lawrence and Beauregard Harden didn't do the dirty deed?"

Okay, so Jane had walked right into that one. "Yes, I can. Their alibis check out one hundred percent."

The reporter perked up. "Do tell. This is the first I've heard about any alibis."

"Well, they both have hearts of gold and morals of steel."

A scowl met her proclamation. "Do you have *concrete* evidence they didn't kill the guy?"

"Do you have concrete evidence that they did?"

Ms. Katz flashed her a gotcha smile and made a notation in her notebook. "So you don't."

Frustrated, Jane demanded, "Tell me their motive."

"All right. Maybe you paid them to do it. This was the third murder to take place on your property. As I mentioned before, you are making a tidy profit from your newfound notoriety."

Maintaining eye contact, Ms. Katz leaned forward. "What about the boost to your romantic life? When Mr. Miller died, you gained another excuse to keep Special Agent Ryan close. A man who may or may not be compromised."

All right. Jane bit her tongue until she tasted a tinge of blood. She withdrew a pen and *Truth Be Told* from her purse. Then, she did what she did best. Let wild theories fly. "What would you say to those wondering if you bought stolen drugs from Emma Miller and murdered her ex-husband after he threatened to turn you in? Then you had the audacity to use the tragedy to make a splash with your first published story while also covering your tracks."

"No one wonders that," Ms. Katz snapped. "And if they do, they shouldn't.

Jane batted her lashes, mimicking Beau's housecaptive. "Can you concretely prove it?"

Scowling, Ms. Katz leaned back and crossed her arms over her chest. "I think you need to leave, Miss Ladling."

"Happy to." As Jane stored her things and stood, she said, "Seems like I've got a new angle to investigate."

CHAPTER FOURTEEN

"To win, you've got to be a triple threat. Starved, mean and loud."

Reggie Belfry, self-proclaimed best chef in Georgia. No, the world.

"What am I missing?" Jane muttered as she rolled out her own white board from the back room. After leaving Ms. Katz's office, she'd bought a burner phone, hoping to get into the mastermind of a depraved killer. Now, to remind herself of all the evidence she'd collected.

Rolex lay on the couch. To protest Cartier's absence, he'd gone on a hunger strike. This was hour three. If it lasted much longer, Jane would be forced to take drastic measures!

"Please, don't worry, baby. I'll win Lucy and Cartier back for us," she vowed. "As soon as I solve this murder, they'll be priority one."

Her mind whirled. Emma. Hagger. Belfry. The three with the greatest motive. It had to be one or two or all. Though Jane had begun to doubt that they'd worked together. The trio had done little to protect each other. Rather, they'd done everything they could to implicate each other.

But. There was also Lucy's sighting of Hagger on her walk to Eden Valley. If Jane believed and trusted her, then she had to rule out the lawyer, leaving only Emma and Belfry. Or maybe Emma and one of the doctors. Price and Garcia. Were Emma and Dr. Price dating? Had Dr. Garcia, the nurse's co-worker, aided his friend? He couldn't account for his whereabouts at the time of death.

But. Which of the five knew how to rewire a car's air system?

Although she couldn't be certain the person who'd sabotaged her car had killed Tony. She'd made a lot of enemies lately apparently.

But. Anyone capable of plotting a murder and framing others understood the principle of covering their tracks. One of the reasons Jake Stephenson, the second murderer to hit the streets of Aurelian Hills, had almost gotten away with his crime? He'd worked alone. There'd been nobody to tattle on him. And, really, the fact that Emma had mentioned the Jake Stephenson case at all, even though she'd had no involvement in it, could mean she'd been the one researching his successes and blunders.

Was the nurse truly so cunning that she could scheme every detail in advance? So cold-blooded, she could work to ensure others took the fall? So confident, she could hire two private investigators without fear of getting caught?

Well, lookie there. Jane's own version of the three C's. Cunning, cold-blooded, and confident.

And what of Belfry and the doctors? Were they cunning, cold-blooded, and confident?

Okay. Forget the doctors. They didn't strike her as Triple C-worthy. If she took Ashley Katz's advice and ruled out

Hagger as well, only Emma and Belfry remained. Honestly, Belfry seemed to lack the smarts for a full-blown cover-up.

That left Emma, the ex-wife.

Excitement bloomed as Jane solidified her verdict. Yes. Emma Miller. She did it. The nurse *must* be the killer. And she'd probably worked alone. Why risk discovery because of a tattletale partner?

She must have hoped Jane and Katz would muddy the waters by casting suspicion on others. In fact, Emma had probably pointed the reporter in Jane's direction.

Had Emma encouraged the romantic attentions of "hothead" Belfry for the express purpose of stirring trouble between him and Tony? With Belfry's violent temper, it wouldn't take long for people to blame him for any wrongdoing.

Perhaps Emma had *wanted* Tony's investigator to snap pictures of her and her "date" kissing in public. Hadn't Belfry called her a "cold fish in private"? Such visual evidence could rile up the ex-husband so obviously obsessed with her, as well as pin two predators against each other, getting rid of both at once.

Jane could see the headline now: *Two Men Meet in a Cemetery, Only One Walks Away.*

No, that headline needed work. Anyway. If Emma had planned this, she wouldn't have left anything to chance. She would've set up Belfry and committed the crime herself.

Yes. That's it! The pieces were falling into place. The reason Tony possessed two burner phones—one had belonged to Emma. She'd used it to paint her own narrative, perhaps not realizing Tony was doing the same. Or she'd painted two different narratives, again to muddy the waters.

No doubt she'd bought Belfry a ticket to the party, not knowing Tony had purchased another. Or she'd bought both.

Emma could have pretended to be Tony, who was

pretending to be Emma, and texted Belfry, offering sex. What perfect Belfry bait. Something only Emma would know? Or was it a guy thing?

Emma could have stashed the burner phone in Tony's pocket after she'd killed him. First, beating him with the rocks, then injecting him with the drug she'd stolen to finish the job.

Or Tony had filched the opioid, thinking to harm or blame Emma and/or Belfry...and use it the same night Emma planned to kill him.

Now there was some pizazz!

Yeah, Emma absolutely positively *must* be the culprit. And oh man, sixty-six percent of the medical staff at the Aurelian Hills Medical Clinic were absolute monsters. First Caroline Whittington, the physician assistant, had killed Dr. Hots and now Nurse Emma had offed her ex-husband.

The doorbell rang, and Jane yelped, yanked out of her head. She checked the time. Yikes! A little after 5:00. She'd pondered the case longer than she'd realized. But at least she'd figured things out!

After shoving the rollaway board back into the office, she sauntered to the door. Her jaw dropped when she spied her visitor through the peephole. Kicking into warp speed, she ripped open the entrance.

"Hi," she croaked, emotion clogging her throat.

"Hi," Lucy said with a half-smile and a weak wave. Cartier's carrier hung over her shoulder. "May we come in?"

"Yes! I mean, if you'd like to, please do." As Jane stepped aside, Rolex jumped from the couch and darted over.

In the carrier, Cartier batted at the walls, attempting to tear free.

The moment the front door snicked shut, Lucy worked to unzip the carrier. The chonky furball erupted from a small opening, and the two felines rubbed together like reunited soul mates, purring.

Tears gathered in the corners of Jane's eyes. Not hugging her visitor required every ounce of her strength. "I'm so happy to see you."

Lucy hooked a lock of hair behind her ear, a little shy and a lot nervous. "I came to say thank you. I'm told you're the one who sent Holden to Oliver," she added at Jane's confused look.

"Dang him! He was supposed to wait for me."

"Well." Her cheeks pinkened. "I'm going on a date with him. Holden, I mean. Not Oliver. Holden, um, explained some things about your investigative process, and how it's a total compliment to slide down your suspect list once your name is on it. Something that's never been done before."

"I'm so sorry I ever doubted you, Lucy. I truly am." The words burst from her. "I've never really had a girlfriend before, and I guess I let fear get the better of me a time or twenty, convincing me that such a new and wonderful part of my life could never last." Perhaps like something she did with another fear…

"I think I had the same reaction." Dark eyes glassed over, tears welling in the corners. "I've had so many things go wrong lately, and then suddenly, I was having fun again and I got scared that it would all crash and burn like everything else, so I bolted at the first opportunity, and I'm sorry I'm rambling right now but this is important so I'm trying to make sure I don't leave anything out."

Okay, Jane couldn't hold out a moment longer. She threw her arms around the other woman and hugged her tight. To her immense delight, Lucy hugged her back. They both laughed and suddenly the world just seemed brighter.

"I think I've solved Tony's murder," Jane told her, excitement shoving the admission off her tongue.

Lucy gaped at her. "Truly?"

She nodded, all but bubbling over. "Want to see how I did it?" Without waiting for a response, she rushed to bring out the board. "I'm almost certain Emma Miller is a lying murderess. Now I just have to gather the evidence to prove it."

In a daze, Lucy studied the scribbled phrases, photos and maze of colorful strings tying everything together. "Oh! I never told you I saw him on my walk to Eden Valley," she said, pointing to Hagger, one of only three photos Jane hadn't yet crossed out. "I encountered so many new faces that day, I'd forgotten him until Ashley Katz ambushed me and shoved his photo in my face."

Knew there was a solid explanation! "I want this case wrapped up in a nice, pink bow, all suspicions lifted off you, Beau and Fiona." The best way to do that? "Obviously, I've got to trap Emma into making a confession."

Jane paced before the board. Back and forth, back and forth. Thinking aloud, she said, "Emma is a player. This was a game of gravestones to her. Too bad the gravekeeper takes the grim reaper. She might have spun a web of smoke and mirrors, and I might be mixing too many metaphors, but I'm going to come in like a wrecking ball."

Lucy tapped her chin, then nodded. "I'm liking where this is headed."

"What if I make her think she made a huge misstep? Left a piece of evidence behind, maybe? Or. Hmm. Emma believed there were no cameras in the Valley of Dolls. What if I can prove her wrong, making her believe—" Oh, oh, oh! Ideas flooded Jane. Now that she'd stopped questioning herself, nothing blocked her creative spirit and flare for drama.

Conrad wasn't going to be happy about any of this. He might even call some of it "illegal" and demand that she stand down. The very reason she would not be telling him about this, either.

Almost giddy, she said, "Give me a minute to make sure my number one idea can work before I dazzle you with my brilliance."

She rushed to her cell phone and texted Beau.

Jane: *Hey! First, you and Sora are so cute together.*

Beaudyguard: *We are NOT together.*

Jane: *Your vehemence is even cuter. Second, don't ask why, but do you know anyone who can expertly manipulate a photo? Like, make it look SUPER real even though it's fake.*

Beaudyguard: Yeah. *Trick. That's how he got his nickname. WHY? What are you planning, Jane?*

Jane ignored Beau's questions and sent a quick message to Trick.

Jane: *Hey, Trick! Jane here. I'd love to bake that casserole for you tonight as well as a dessert. I won't mention it to any of your friends so you can enjoy every bite yourself...in exchange for your speediest photo manipulation skills. The end result MUST look real. Even though one of the images you'll be working with comes from video surveillance at the Garden.*

Trickster: *Not a problem. Tell me what you want done, and I'll have something back to you the second that casserole and dessert come out of the oven. I promise you, the photo will pass any inspection.*

Jane: *Grab an image of Emma Miller the night of the party. Place her near a shot of Tony's body (from the crime scene photos on Beau's phone). Maybe put a bag of gold in her hand? I'll leave the finer details up to you. See you in two hours!*

"Okay, I don't even know what's going on, but this is just so exciting," Lucy said, clapping.

"It really, really is." She took Lucy's hand and led her friend into the kitchen. "Come on."

Once the other woman settled in at the counter, Jane

prepared them both a glass of sweet tea and strapped on an apron.

"Well?" Lucy squealed. "Tell me everything!"

As Jane gathered ingredients for Trick's casserole and dessert, she explained, "Okay. Get this. I'm gonna make Emma think someone took a photo of her when she killed Tony. She'll see the image and panic. I'll tell her she can buy my silence. We'll meet, and I'll trick her into making a confession."

"I love it. But what if she attacks you to keep you quiet? And won't she realize this is a setup? You aren't exactly the blackmailing type. And what if she's innocent and calls the cops?" Lucy pressed a hand over her heart. "Jane, you could be arrested and sent to prison!"

"That's a risk I'm willing to take to clear my innocent friends. And also for justice or whatever."

"But Rolex." Lucy waved to the table. "He would be devastated without you."

Jane glanced over to see her precious angel baby curled up in the centerpiece bowl, with Cartier snuggled in beside him. "Yes," she said with her driest tone, "I'm sure he'll be shattered."

Lucy followed her line of sight and giggled. "If you're positive you want to do this, I'm totally willing to help. Put me in the game, coach. I'm ready to come off the bench."

Laughing, Jane prepped the chicken with a creamy marinade. "I'm not sure what to do about the meet up."

"I know there's a solution. It's right there at the edge of my brain, waiting to be discovered." Lucy thought for a moment before brightening. "I've got it! Tiffany Hotchkins is throwing a costume party this weekend. I see her flyer every time I step in the office. Well, what if you somehow keep your identity a secret and suggest Emma meet you there? Even an evil murderess is less likely to strike in public."

"Yes!" How utterly perfect. This might turn out to be Jane's biggest bust yet.

"As for the money," the other woman continued, "you should demand at least fifty thousand."

What! "So much? She'll never be able to put together such a large sum so quickly. She might decide to skip town rather than meet with me."

"Trust me." Lucy gave her a pointed look. "She can afford it, Jane."

Had she gotten a big settlement from Tony, despite rumors? And the loan officer knew this because she had access to the other woman's account?

Well. Having friends rocked! As the rice softened, Jane grated different cheeses and brainstormed the perfect wordage to accompany Trick's photo. Lucy helped but jetted off about half an hour before the vet's scheduled arrival, promising to call in the morning. She took Cartier with her, and Rolex pouted. Jane shared chicken with him to lift his spirit.

The remaining time flew by, and all too soon both the dish and the dessert were done, and the man of the hour was ringing her doorbell.

Brimming with excitement, she welcomed Trick inside. His eyes closed. He moaned as he sniffed the aromatic air. "Tonight I feast."

"Payment first," she said.

He whipped out his phone, telling her, "Here's the photo. No need to tell me how good I am. I *know*."

Her cell vibrated in her pocket as she led him to the kitchen, where he dove into the casserole with great enthusiasm.

Tremors struck her as she checked the image—wow, wow, wow! It really did appear authentic. He had exceeded her expectations. Emma stood behind the body, one foot in front of the other, as if she prepared to flee. Her expression hovered somewhere between determined and angry.

"Don't tell me what you're planning," Trick said, just before shoveling in another bite.

"Okay. I won't." She forwarded the photo to her new burner phone. Stomach churning, she typed the message she and Lucy had crafted.

EMMA MILLER. I KNOW WHAT YOU DID. IF YOU DON'T WANT OTHERS TO KNOW YOU'LL BRING 50K TO THE HOTCHKINS PARTY. I'LL ISSUE FURTHER INSTRUCTIONS THERE.

And...send.

Now, Jane waited.

JANE REMAINED on edge the rest of the evening, staring at the burner phone, desperate to receive a response.

She brushed her teeth, preparing for bed. Still waiting.

Climbed under the covers and settled in. Still waiting.

At least Rolex cuddled up to her, back to his old self. He knew he'd get to see his girlfriend again. Life was good —for him.

Still waiting.

At precisely 2:46 a.m. Jane's burner phone beeped. She jolted upright and swung the little device in front of her face to check the screen. Three words peered up at her, making her heart leap.

I'll be there.

CHAPTER FIFTEEN

"I'd rather eat a nail than accept a participation trophy."
Conrad Ryan, special agent at Georgia Bureau of Homicide

"All right. I've got eyes on Emma." Beau's husky voice poured through the device he'd plugged into Jane's ear before he'd left the cottage earlier. He'd dubbed himself "central command," his job to maintain contact with every Team Truth player in tonight's game. "She's in the backyard, dressed as a spy and carrying a briefcase. She's definitely agitated and on high alert."

Heart thumping, Jane glanced at Conrad, who sat behind the wheel of his sedan with a device in his ear, as well. "You ready?" she asked from the passenger side.

"No, but I guess we're doing this, anyway." He exited the vehicle with a huff, and Jane sighed.

Her boys were in no way pleased with her and her plan. But they'd recognized brilliance when they'd heard it...after a couple hours of convincing on her part. On their part, she'd received countless lectures about never again putting herself in danger.

As she double checked the contents of her pink jelly-purse—a vintage find at a thrift store—Conrad jogged around the vehicle, opened her door and extended a helping hand. Emerging into the night, she adjusted her single, fingerless glove. With her legwarmers, lacy miniskirt, and layered pearls, Jane felt ready to conquer the world. The neck of her T-shirt hung off one shoulder, and it was totally tubular. Like beyond tripendicular. Most triumphant. Whatever!

She'd begun this latest investigation in the 1920s, but would finish it as an 80s fashion icon. Conrad's costume? A plain white T-shirt and gray sweatpants. He'd said, "Consider me an advertisement for men's lounge wear."

Granted, he looked as hot as ever. If not hotter. Okay, so, definitely hotter. The definition!

Her cheeks grew hot as they strolled down the darkened street toward Tiffany's three-story mansion. Eerie lights and creepy decorations lined the long, winding driveway.

"I don't want you putting yourself in danger," he said for the thousandth time.

"Conrad. Sweet pea." No, that was in no way the perfect nickname for him. She'd try a new one later. "When you're doing the right thing, it isn't dangerous, it's righteous. So get on the rightness train and hold on or get off at the next stop. Your choice."

He scowled at her. "You are not to leave my side," he informed her, taking her hand.

Goodness gracious! "For this to work, I *have* to leave your side. Emma won't pay up if you're nearby. Deep down, you know this. It's why you're willing to go along. That, and your boss gave us the green light. Plus, you'll hear me the entire time." Before they left the cottage, he'd activated their shared phone app. "Also, I'll never be without protection. The members of Peach State Security are already mingling with party guests." Even Fiona and a much recovered Sheriff

Moore had come. Deputies, too. And Lucy! This was a bona fide sting operation, with local cops and GBH agents mixed into the crowd!

Tiffany's front door remained wide open. Conrad muttered, "Let's get this done," and ushered Jane inside the home.

Fast-paced music played in the background. On one side, strobe lights tossed shards of color around and around. On the other, a thin layer of fog wafted from a machine. Lifelike bats dangled from the ceiling. And oh, they were adorable. Like little sky kittens.

Laughing adults filled the foyer, some dancing. Others huddled together and sipped their beverages. Their costumes varied from sexy to scary, elaborate to simple. Jane recognized most of the guests. Those sporting masks remained a mystery, however.

"By the way, Jane," Beau muttered in her ear. "I can't believe you talked me into wearing this abomination. Trick hasn't stopped snickering. Isaac took my picture and vowed to post it everywhere, and Holden says he can never take me seriously again."

She stifled a chuckle, and even Conrad cracked a smile. Had she jumped on the opportunity to dress Beau as a sexy vampire, complete with a purple velvet duster, black leather pants and body glitter? Yes. Did she allow him to add a shirt to the ensemble? No. Did she regret it? Also no. Not the slightest bit.

"Did Sora like it?" she asked softly, knowing her friend could hear every word.

"She was too busy making strangling noises to tell me. And that's the last question I'll answer about her."

Jane couldn't see him, but she imagined his cheeks were a brighter pink than her glove.

"Jane Ladling, as I live and breathe. How dare you show your face here?" Tiffany Hotchkins marched over, dressed in what could only be described as a mantrap fairy. She wore a front-tie corset dress in ruby red and thigh-high stiletto boots, with ornate sequined wings stretching over her shoulders. "You need to leave. Now."

"But I'm not Jane Ladling today," she replied, spreading her arms. "I'm a simple valley girl."

"You told Sheriff Moore you'd like law enforcement present tonight," Conrad said. "Well, I'm here. With my plus one."

Tiffany's expression veered from furious to indigent before she refocused her ire on Jane. "If you accuse one guest of murder…if anyone *gets* murdered, I'll…I'll…Just behave!" She stomped off.

With an arm draped around Jane's waist, Conrad led her to the vast sitting area. "First hurdle has been cleared," he muttered.

Wait staff flitted about, carrying trays of Halloween themed foods. Severed finger sandwiches. Spider pizza bites. Meatball mummies.

Don't mind if I do. Jane plucked up several of the sandwiches. Mmm. So good!

"Focus, sweetheart." He didn't attempt to hide his amusement. "Blackmail first. Snacks second. When this is over, and you are completely unharmed, I will provide you with a feast."

The promise in his voice left her shivering.

They continued through the house, now void of any of the "artwork" Tiffany once proudly displayed for her murderous boyfriend. Jane spotted both Berdize sisters, directing traffic and totally in their element. Oh! There was Trick, mingling with Ashley Katz. He wore a cowboy hat and boots like he was born for the saddle. The reporter, dressed as a seductive cat, didn't look as if she would mind being lassoed.

He winked when Jane and Conrad passed him. Ms. Katz merely arched a brow.

They entered the backyard, where plastic bodies floated across a kidney-shaped pool. Pumpkins and hay bales complimented the stunning, all-weather landscaping. Tiki torches provided plenty of illumination as a projector cast dancing ghosts and creepy crawlers along the shadowy walls of the pool house. The scent of clashing perfumes and citrus fruit saturated the chilly air.

Finally, Jane spotted the rest of her group. Isaac, who'd come as a medieval prince, sported armor and a crown. He was currently charming a cluster of older women from a wellness center Fiona frequented.

Holden came dressed as a Viking—at Jane's suggestion, thank you—with straps of brown leather crossed over his broad, muscular chest. But it was Lucy as a valkyrie, complete with sleek body armor and a spear, who stole the show. So fierce!

They were, like, the world's most adorable couple.

They stood with the sheriff and Fiona, who'd come decked out as pirates.

Fiona winked at Jane. Lucy rested her head on Holden's shoulder and smiled, giving Jane a stealthy thumbs up.

No sign of Beau, though. Her heart started thumping again when she spotted Emma, clad in a long trench coat—well able to hide weapons—holding a briefcase no doubt filled with cash. She stood with Dr. Price, Dr. Garcia and Devin Hagger. Well, well, well. What a foursome.

Building another false narrative, hoping to silence her blackmailer for good?

Too bad. Soon, the truth would come out. According to the plan, Jane would let the nurse sweat for an hour and maybe throw back a couple drinks to calm her nerves. Then, Jane would get in position and shoot Emma a message from the burner, telling her to leave the money in Tiffany's private bathroom, where—surprise—Jane would be waiting.

"Emma's on the move," Beau announced in her ear. "Headed to the bar."

Jane glanced over and sure enough, the nurse crossed to the wet bar, where a waiter served bloody marys.

Sipping her drink, Emma joined one group after another, chatting and laughing as if she hadn't a care. But she continually checked her phone, clearly waiting for a certain message…

When she disappeared inside the pool house, Beau said, "Holden, send Fiona and Lucy in to keep an eye on our spy."

Jane's nerves sharpened when the girls followed Emma.

Only a few minutes later, Beau's voice sounded in her ear. "Emma stored her briefcase inside. Apparently, Tiffany rented a bank of lockers for the event."

Emma strutted from the pool house in the coat—which she removed as she walked, revealing a red bikini. The cell phone remained clutched in her hand as she waded into the heated pool and socialized with the handful of other swimming guests.

At first glance, she seemed to be having a wonderful time. At second, Jane noted the brittleness of her smile.

Finally, the moment for action arrived. Jane and Conrad ventured inside the house. Holden, Lucy, Fiona, and the sheriff kept Tiffany busy. Conrad, Trick and Isaac snuck Jane into the restricted—and locked—master suite. The site of her coming crime. Well, almost. But oh, wow, the bedroom really made a statement. It said: *I'm rich.* With its carved bed frame of deep mahogany, the softest of the soft jewel-toned bedding—and yes, she stroked her hand along the silk to verify her assessment—and a sitting area arranged before a modern, landscape fireplace, this was a room for dreams.

"Be careful," Conrad said, planting a swift kiss on her lips. "I mean it. When this is over, there better not be a scratch on you."

Breathless, she told him, "Same to you, officer detective."

"Don't forget inspector. But I prefer sweet pea." He gave her another kiss, and then he was gone.

To stealthily check Emma for weapons, Conrad would be "accidentally" bumping into her before she entered the bedroom to make the payment. He would also be asking her if she'd seen a missing Jane, making it clear he wasn't hiding in wait, ready to overhear a confession, as soon as she discovered the true identify of her blackmailer.

Jane had to admit she loved the drama of it all.

Smiling, she shut herself in the cavernous bathroom with gold and crystal fixtures, steam shower and floor to ceiling mirrors. Trick and Isaac took up posts inside the closet.

"I'm sending the message," she told Conrad and Beau through the microphone. Her hand trembled as she withdrew the burner from her pocket and typed: YOU HAVE 3 MINUTES BRING THE MONEY TO TIFF'S PERSONAL BATHROOM. CLOCK STARTS NOW.

"And...send," she rasped. Gah! This was really happening.

Only a split second afterward, Beau announced, "Emma just saw the message. She's pale as a ghost and racing back into the pool house... now she's racing out with the case in hand."

It was working! Perspiration dotted Jane's palms.

Rocking her weight from one foot to the other, she waited. Moments later, hinges sounded, followed by rushing footsteps. Then Emma burst into the bathroom. She stopped short when she spotted Jane, a myriad of emotions contorting her face. Surprise. Worry. Resentment.

"You," the nurse spat.

"Yes. Me." Jane easily slipped into character. Greedy wench with a taste for the highlife.

"I *knew* you weren't the sweetheart you pretended to be."

Okay, now that might have stung a bit. "Where's my money?"

"You already got it," was the screeched reply. "I'm not paying you twice."

Jane scowled at her. "I didn't tell you to pay me twice. I told you to pay me now. Give me my money, and we go our separate ways. I'll forget I even have such an incriminating photo of you."

"Liar! You texted and told me there'd been a change of plans, and I was to leave the case in a locker. Which I did." Emma tore open the briefcase. "As you can see, it's empty. The money is gone."

Jane blinked at her. "I *never* told you to leave the case in a locker."

"You did! And I obeyed." The nurse tossed the case at Jane's feet. "I've followed each instruction to the letter. Why is everyone always trying to screw me over? First Tony, now you."

Finally! Her chance to coax a confession. "Please! You brought this on yourself. You didn't have to kill Tony, but you did."

"Of course I did! He did everything in his power to ruin my life, and Reggie's temper didn't do the job. All I wanted was to start a new life with Freddie in peace."

Freddie. As in Dr. Frederick Price? So they *were* dating.

"Tony stole drugs from the hospital, planning to frame

me and get me fired. He bragged about it," Emma sneered. "What was I supposed to do? Let him?"

Well. That explained a lot. "You think that excuses your actions? You could have gone to Sheriff Moore, explained what was going on. He would have helped you handle things legally."

The other woman scrunched her face up tight. "Maybe I would have. But the night of your party, Tony noticed the way I looked at Freddie and threatened to blame him for the stolen drugs. I told him we'd talk in the Valley of Dolls. Then I spotted the bag of gold and…reacted."

"Maybe you seized upon the weapon, but you planned everything else. After you hit him and injected him with the opioid, making sure he died, you planted a burner phone in his pocket," Jane said. *I got it right, didn't I?* "What I want to know is why you hired me."

Emma jerked back. "Why else? You were supposed to do your thing, suspecting everyone of everything, throwing around your wild theories and generally confusing things."

Another stinger. Though, perhaps, a tad bit accurate. "Why mess with my car, then? I love that hearse."

"I didn't touch your car, so don't even think about blaming me. I won't be paying for damages. Now, you're going to delete that photo while I watch, Jane, or I swear you'll suffer the same fate as Tony. I'll make sure your boyfriend is blamed. Only takes a little planning and misdirection."

Um, did that count as a full-on confession? It must not, otherwise Conrad would've burst into the bathroom with handcuffs at the ready. "First of all, I won't go down as easily as Tony. Second, you're not bluffing your way out of paying me." She pinched her features into her fiercest expression. "Give me. My money. Now!"

"You think Tony went down easy?" Snorting, Emma took a step closer. "I had to hit him and hit him and hit him. Now you delete that photo—"

The door burst open, and yep, Conrad stormed inside with cuffs. Holden charged in behind him. Trick and Isaac sprang from the closet, the group quickly surrounding the nurse.

When Emma attempted to flee, Conrad snagged her by the waist. The two grappled to the floor, but he had no trouble locking her arms behind her back and clicking the cuffs in place. And just like that, the case of the Nasty Nurse and the Lowly Lawyer was closed.

Jane pumped both fists to the ceiling. "I did it! I saved the day, served justice on ice and outwitted a criminal mastermind with a simple plan."

"Except Emma wasn't lying," Beau said in her ear, his tone far from jubilant. "The money's gone—and so is Lucy."

JANE and the rest of Team Truth crammed into Conrad's office in Atlanta. After the nurse's arrest, they'd all come in to give their statements. Jane hadn't stopped reeling. She'd gained a confession, solving Tony's murder, but she'd also lost her first girlfriend.

Lucy had indeed run off with Emma's money. Not that anyone could prove it. Emma's confiscated phone confirmed the texts she'd mentioned—from a burner phone that did not belong to Jane.

"Lucy owned a burner of her own," Trick said, and Holden flinched.

"She distracted Fiona in the pool house and grabbed the

cash. I'm not sure how she hid it," Holden said, grim. "When I followed Conrad into the house, she ran."

Perhaps never to be seen or heard from again.

And Jane had thought her gut beyond reproach. How could she have been fooled so easily? How could she have been so wrong about someone? And why would Lucy steal the money? Fifty thousand wasn't much to live on. Not for long anyway. Would she return to town?

Jane slumped in her chair. Lucy's love for Cartier had blinded her to the truth, most likely. Unless she'd left the cat behind? Speaking of animals, what would happen to Emma's dog, Cheddar?

Beside her, Fiona reached over and squeezed her hand. "It's gonna be all right, hon."

Yeah, she had to pull it together. "We may have to rescue a dog and a cat after this," she muttered.

"Not the cat," Holden said. "I stopped at Lucy's before coming here, and she'd already packed up the cat and some clothes and blazed."

Poor Rolex. "Did Dr. Price know about Emma's homicidal side?"

"Doesn't seem like it," Conrad replied. "He believed Tony might hurt her and followed him to act as her protection. She ensured Dr. Price got busy with something else before she went after Tony."

"I'm retiring," Sheriff Moore announced without warning. He stood behind Fiona, his hands resting on her shoulders. "Effective immediately."

Fiona nodded and patted his fingers, as if she'd known this was coming.

What? No! No, no, no. "What is Aurelian Hills supposed to do without you?" Jane cried.

His expression remained hard as granite as he motioned to Conrad. "Your turn, Ryan. Tell them."

Wait. What? Eyes wide, she darted her gaze to her special agent city boy. "Tell us what?"

He glowered at the sheriff. "This isn't the way we talked about making such a big announcement."

Sheriff Moore shrugged. "Plans change, son. Roll with it."

"This is our cue," Beau said, shooing everyone toward the door. "Let's go."

Jane and Fiona shared a concerned look before the grandmother left with the group, leaving Jane alone with Conrad. They peered at each other from across the desk, her ability to breathe deserting her bit by bit.

"I've thought about this a lot," he said, tapping the edge of a pen on the desk's surface. "I'll be moving to Aurelian Hills and running for the position of sheriff."

A choking sound left her. Not a city boy anymore? But a —gulp—local? *Breathe. Just breathe.*

"Face it, Jane. Your town is a hotbed of crime. Lucy will return, guaranteed. And we still don't know who sabotaged your car. The innocent citizens of Aurelian Hills deserve a police force up to the task. Ms. Miller doesn't have any family, so she asked me to find a good home for Cheddar. I am that home. We both know there's no better place to raise a pet."

"But…" What defense would Jane have against Conrad and his charming ways now?

He stood and walked around the desk, then took her hands and drew her to her feet. As she straightened, he sat at the edge and pulled her against him. She didn't fight the contact. No, she sank into him.

"You're welcoming our doom," she whispered, playing with the neckline of his shirt.

"No, sweetheart." He shook his head. "I'm giving us a real chance. I love you, Jane Ladling, and I'm never letting you go."

Up Next:

Twelve Graves of Christmas

A Christmas novella in the Jane Ladling Mystery Series

ABOUT GENA SHOWALTER

Gena Showalter is the New York Times and USA TODAY bestselling author of multiple "unputdownable" series in paranormal, contemporary, and young adult romance.

Learn more about Gena, her menagerie of rescue dogs, and all her upcoming books at genashowalter.com

ALSO BY GENA SHOWALTER

Immortal Enemies

Start with: Heartless

.

Rise of the Warlords

Start with: The Warlord

.

Lords of the Underworld

Start with: The Darkest Night

.

White Rabbit Chronicles

Start with: Alice in Zombieland

.

Tales of an Extraordinary Girl

Start with: Playing with Fire

.

Everlife

Start with: Firstlife

.

Original Heartbreakers

Start with: The Secret Fling

.

Angels of the Dark:

Start with: Wicked Nights

.

Otherworld Assassins

Start with: Last Kiss Goodnight

·

Non-Fiction:

(Co-written with Jill Monroe)

All Write Already

All Write Already Workbook

The Write Life

Write Now! An All Write Already Journal

·

Gena's Complete List of Releases:

GenaShowalter.com/books

ABOUT JILL MONROE

Jill Monroe is the international best selling author of over fifteen novels and novellas. Her books are available across the globe and ***The Wrong Bed: Naked Pursuit*** has been adapted for the small screen for Lifetime Movie Network.

When not writing, Jill makes her home in Oklahoma with her husband, enjoys daily walks with her dog Zoey, texting with her two daughters who are away at college and collecting fabric for items she'll sew poorly.

Learn more about Jill at jillmonroe.com

ALSO BY JILL MONROE

Sworn Series:

Sworn Promises

Sworn Duty

Sworn By A Kiss

Sworn Protector

.

Wrong Bed Series

Naked Thrill

Naked Pursuit*

*(Now a movie from Lifetime Movie Network)

.

From Hallmark:

At The Heart of Christmas

.

Non-Fiction:

(Co-written with Gena Showalter)

All Write Already

All Write Already Workbook

The Write Life

Write Now! An All Write Already Journal

.

Jill's Complete List of Releases:

https://jillmonroe.com/allbooks/

Printed in Poland
by Amazon Fulfillment
Poland Sp. z o.o., Wrocław

23870833R00109